MR TRILL IN HADES
& other stories

BY THE SAME AUTHOR:

Fiction

CONSIDER THE LILIES

THE LAST SUMMER

SURVIVAL WITHOUT ERROR
(short stories)

THE BLACK AND THE RED
(short stories)

MY LAST DUCHESS

GOODBYE, MR DIXON

THE HERMIT AND OTHER STORIES

AN END TO AUTUMN

MURDO AND OTHER STORIES
(short stories)

A FIELD FULL OF FOLK

THE SEARCH

Poetry

FROM BOURGEOIS LAND

LOVE POEMS AND ELEGIES

SELECTED POEMS

NOTEBOOKS OF ROBINSON CRUSOE

IN THE MIDDLE

THE EXILES

MR TRILL IN HADES
& *other stories*

by

IAIN CRICHTON SMITH

LONDON
VICTOR GOLLANCZ LTD
1984

"What to do about Ralph?" has previously appeared in *Shakespeare Stories* edited by Giles Gordon and published by Hamish Hamilton.

British Library Cataloguing in Publication Data
Smith, Iain Crichton
    Mr Trill in Hades and other stories.
    I. Title
    823'.914[F]   PR6005.R58

    ISBN 0-575-03417-3

Photoset in Great Britain by
Photobooks (Bristol) Ltd
and printed by
St Edmundsbury Press, Bury St Edmunds, Suffolk

CONTENTS

WHAT TO DO ABOUT RALPH?

"WHAT ON EARTH has happened to you?" said his mother. "These marks are getting worse and worse. I thought with your father teaching you English you might have done better."

"He is not my father," Ralph shouted, "he is not my father."

"Of course, having you in class is rather awkward but you should be more helpful than you are. After all, you are seventeen. I shall have to speak to him about these marks."

"It won't do any good."

How sullen and stormy he always was these days, she thought, it's such a constant strain. Maybe if he went away to university there might be some peace.

"He has been good to you, you know; he has tried," she continued. But Ralph wasn't giving an inch. "He bought you all that football stuff and the hi-fi and the portable TV."

"So I could keep out of his road, that's why."

"You know perfectly well that's not true."

"It is true. And anyway, I didn't want him here. We could have been all right on our own."

How could she tell him that to be on your own was not easy? She had jumped at the chance of getting out of teaching and, in any case, they were cutting down on Latin teachers nowadays. Furthermore, the pupils, even the academic ones, were becoming more difficult. She had been very lucky to have had the chance of marrying again, after the hard years with Tommy. But you couldn't tell Ralph the truth about Tommy, he wouldn't listen. Most people, including Ralph, had seen Tommy as cheerful, humorous, generous, only she knew what he had been really like. Only she knew, as well, the incredible jealousy that had existed between Jim and Tommy from their youth. Almost pathological, especially on Tommy's side. It was as if they had never had any love from their professor father who had been cold and remote, hating the noise of children in the house. They had competed for what few scraps of love he had been able to throw to them now and again.

She couldn't very well tell Ralph that the night his father had crashed his car he had been coming from another woman, on Christmas Eve. She had been told that in the wrecked car the radio was playing 'Silent Night'.

Of course, in his own field Tommy had been quite good, at least at the beginning. He had been given a fair number of parts in the Theatre and later some minor ones on TV. But then he had started drinking as the depression gripped and the parts became smaller and less frequent. His downfall had been his golden days at school when he had been editor of the magazine, captain of the rugby team, actor. What a hero he had been in those days, how invisible Jim had been. And even now invisible in Ralph's eyes. And he had been invisible to her as well, though she often recalled the night when Tommy had gate crashed Jim's birthday party and had got drunk and shouted that he would stab him. But he had been very drunk that night. "I'll kill you," he had shouted. Why had he hated Jim so much even though on the surface he himself had been the more successful of the two? At least at the beginning?

She should have married Jim in the first place; she could see that he was much kinder than Tommy, less glamorous, less loved by his father, insofar as there had been much of that. But she had been blinded by Tommy's apparent brilliance and humour, and, to tell the truth, by his more blatant sexiness.

Of course he had never had any deep talent, his handsomeness had been a sort of compensatory glow, but when that faded everything else faded too. She herself had been too complaisant, declining to take the hard decision of leaving him, still teaching in those days, and tired always.

To Ralph, however, his father had appeared different. He had been the one who carried him about on his shoulders, taught him how to ride a motor bike, how to play snooker (had even bought a snooker table for him), taken him to the theatre to see him perform. Even now his photograph was prominent in his son's room. She had been foolish to hide from him the true facts about his father's death, his drunken crash when returning home from one of his one-night stands. She should have told him the truth, but she hadn't. She had always taken the easy way out, though in fact it wasn't in the end the easy way at all.

And then Jim had started to visit her, he now a promoted teacher, although in the days when Tommy had been alive not often seen except casually at teachers' conferences, but very correct, stiffly lonely, and certainly not trying to come between her and his brother, though she knew that he had always liked her. She had learned in the interval that kindness was more important than glamour, for glamour meant that others demanded some of your light, that you belonged as much to the public as to your wife. Or so Tommy had used to say.

She remembered with distaste the night of the school play when she had played the virginal Ophelia to his dominating Hamlet, off-hand, negligent, hurtful, almost as if he really believed what he was saying to her. But the dazzled audience had clapped and clapped, and even the professor father had turned up to see the theatrical life and death of his son.

But how to tell Ralph all this?

That night she said to Jim in bed,

"What are we going to do about Ralph?"

"What now?"

"You've seen his report card? He used to be a bright boy. I'm not just saying that. His marks are quite ridiculous. Can't you give him some help in the evenings? English used to be his best subject. In primary school he was always top."

"I can help him if he'll take it. But he won't take it. His English is ludicrous."

"Ludicrous? What do you mean?"

"What I said. Ludicrous." And then, of course, she had defended Ralph. No one was going to say to her that her son's intellect was ludicrous which she knew it wasn't. And so it all began again, the argument that never ended, that wasn't the fault of anyone in particular, but only of the situation that seemed to be insoluble, for Ralph was the thorn at their side, sullen, implacable, unreachable.

"I'm afraid he hates me and that's it," said Jim. "To tell you the truth, I think he has been very ungrateful."

She could see that herself, but at the same time she could see Ralph's side of it too.

"Ungrateful?" she said.

'Yes. Ungrateful. You remember the time I got so angry that I told him I had after all brought him a television set and he shouted, 'You're a bloody fool then.'"

"You have to try and understand him," she said.

"It's always the same. He won't make the effort to understand. His father's the demi-god, the hero. If he only knew what a bastard he really was." Always making fun of him with his quick tongue, always taking girls away from him, always lying to his distant father about him, always making him appear the slow resentful one.

That night she slept fitfully. She had the feeling that something terrible was happening, that something even more terrible was about to happen. And always Ralph sat in his room playing his barbarous music very loudly. His stepfather would mark his eternal essays in his meticulous red writing, she would sew, and together they sat in the living room hearing the music till eventually he would tell her to go and ask Ralph to turn it down. She it was who was always the messenger between them, the ambassador trying hopelessly to reconcile but never succeeding. For Ralph resented her now as much as he resented Jim.

She couldn't believe that this could go on.

Ralph sat at the back of his stepfather's class, contemptuous, remote, miserable. Quite apart from the fact that he thought him boring, he was always being teased by the other pupils about him. His nickname was Sniffy, for he had a curious habit of sniffing now and again as if there was a bad smell in the room. But, to be fair to him, he was a good, conscientious teacher: he set homework and marked it and it really seemed as if he wanted them all to pass. But there was a curious remoteness to him, as if he loved his subject more than he loved them. Nevertheless, he was diligent and he loved literature.

"This, of course, was the worst of crimes," he was saying, sitting at his desk in his chalky gown. "We have to remember that this was a brother who killed another one, like Cain killing Abel. Then again there is the murder in the Garden, as if it were the garden of Eden. There is so much religion in the play. Hamlet himself was religious; that, after all, was the reason he didn't commit suicide. Now, there is a very curious question posed by the play, and it is this " (he sniffed again),

"What was going on between Gertrude and Claudius even while the latter's brother Hamlet was alive? This king about whom we know so little. Here's the relevant speech:

> "Aye that incestuous, that adulterate beast,
> with witchcraft of his wit, with traitorous gifts,
> won to his shameful lust
> the will of a most seeming virtuous queen . . ."

The point was, had any of this happened in Hamlet's lifetime? He meant, of course, King Hamlet's. Had there been a liaison between Gertrude and Claudius even then? One got the impression of Claudius being a ladies' man, while Hamlet perhaps was the soldier who blossomed in action, and who was not much concerned with the boudoir. After all, he was a public figure, he perhaps took Gertrude for granted. On their answer to that question would depend their attitude to Gertrude.

The voice droned on, but it was as if a small red window had opened in Ralph's mind. He had never thought before that his mother had known his stepfather before the marriage which had taken place so suddenly. What if in fact there had been something going on between them while his father was still alive? He shivered as if he had been infected by a fever. He couldn't bring himself to think of his mother and stepfather in bed together, which was why he had asked for his own bedroom to be changed, so that he would be as far away from them as possible.

But suppose there had been a liaison between them. After all, they had both been teachers and they must have met. True, they had been at different schools but it was inconceivable that they hadn't met.

O God, how dull his stepfather was, in his cloud of chalk. How different from his father who inhabited the large air of the theatre. What a poor ghostly fellow he was in his white dust.

But the idea that his mother had known his stepfather would not leave his mind. How had he never thought of it before?

That night, his stepfather being at a meeting at the school, he said to his mother,

"Did you know . . . your husband . . . before you married him?"

"I wish you could call him your stepfather, or even refer to him by his first name. Of course I knew him. I knew the family."

"But you married my father?"

"Yes. And listen, Ralph, I have never said this to you before. I made a great mistake in marrying your father."

He was about to rise and leave the room when she said vehemently, "No, it's time you listened. You sit down there and listen for a change. Did you know that your father was a drunk? Do you know that he twice gave me a black eye? The time I told everybody I had cut myself on the edge of the wardrobe during the power cut, and the time I said I had fallen on the ice? Did you know where he was coming from when his car crashed?"

"I don't want to hear any more," Ralph shouted. "If you say any more I'll kill you. It's not true. You're lying."

For a moment there he might have attacked her, he looked so white and vicious. It was the first time he had thought of hitting her; he came very close.

Her face was as pale as his and she was almost swaying on her feet but she was shouting at him,

"He was coming from one of his innumerable lady friends. I didn't tell you that, did I? I got a message from the police and I went along there. He had told me he was going to be working late at the theatre but he was coming from the opposite direction. He was a stupid man. At least Jim is not stupid."

He raised his fist as if to hit her, but she didn't shrink away.

"Go on, hit me," she shouted. "Hit me because you can't stand the truth any more than your father could. He was vulgar, not worth your stepfather's little finger."

He turned and ran out of the house.

Of course it wasn't true. That story was not the one his mother had told him before. And for all he knew the two of them might have killed his father, they might have tampered with the brakes or the engine. After all, a car crash was always suspicious, and his father had been a good if fast driver. His stepfather couldn't even drive.

He went to the Nightspot where some boys from the school were playing snooker, and older ones drinking at the bar. He stood for a while watching Harry and Jimmy playing. Harry had been to college but had given it up and was now on the dole. Jimmy had never left town at all. He watched as Harry hit the assembled balls and sent them flying across the table. After a while he went and sat down by himself. He felt as if he had run away from home, as if he wanted to kill himself. He was tired of always being in the same room by himself playing records. And yet he couldn't bring himself to talk to his stepfather. The two of them were together, had shut him out, he was like a refugee in the house. He hated to watch his stepfather eating, and above all he hated to see him kissing his mother before he set off for school with his briefcase under his arm. But then if he himself left home where could he go? He had no money. He loathed being dependent on them for pocket money, which he used buying records.

He hated his mother as much as he hated his stepfather. At other times he thought that they might have been able to live together, just the two of them, if his stepfather had not appeared. Why, he had loved her in the past and she had loved him, but now she had shut him out because she thought he was being unfair to her husband. He was such a drip: he couldn't play snooker, and all he did was mark essays every night. The house felt cold now, he was rejected, the other two were drawing closer and closer together.

"How's old Sniffy," said Terry as he sat down at the same table, Frank beside him. They, of course, were unemployed and Terry had been inside for nicking stuff and also for nearly killing a fellow at a dance.

Then they began to talk about school and he had to sit and

listen. Terry had once punched Caney and had been dragged away by the police. No one could control him at all. Frank was just as dangerous, but brighter, more cunning.

"Have a whisky," said Terry. "Go on. I bet you've never had a whisky before. I'll buy it for you."

The snooker table with the green baize brought unbearable memories back to him, and he said,

"Right. Right then."

"I'll tell you another thing," said Terry. "Old Sniffy's a poof. I always thought he was a poof. What age was the bugger when he got married? Where was he getting it before that?"

Frank didn't say anything at all, but watched Ralph. He had never liked him. He had belonged to the academic stream while he himself was always in one of the bottom classes, though he was much brighter.

"A poof," Terry repeated. "But he's having it off now, eh, Frank?" And winked at Frank. Ralph drank the whisky in one gulp, and tears burned his eyes.

"Old bastard," said Terry. "He belted me a few times and I wasn't even in his class."

The two of them took Ralph back to his house. Then they stood around it for a while shouting at the lighted window, "Sniffy the Poof, Sniffy the Poof." And then ran away into the darkness. Ralph staggered to his room.

"What was that? Who was shouting there?" said his mother. "Some of your friends. You're drunk. You're disgustingly drunk."

But he pushed her away and went to his bed while the walls and ceiling spun about him and the bed moved up and down like a boat beneath him.

He heard his mother shouting at his stepfather, "What are you going to do about it then? You can't sit here and do nothing. He's drunk, I'm telling you. Will you give up those exercise books and do something?"

Later he heard his mother slamming the door and heard the car engine start, then he fell into a deep sleep.

At breakfast no one spoke. It was like a funeral. He himself had a terrible headache, like a drill behind his right eye, and he felt awful. His mother stared down at the table. His stepfather didn't kiss her when he left for school: he seemed preoccupied and pale. It was as if the house had come to a complete stop, as if it had crashed.

"You have to remember," said his stepfather when talking about *Hamlet* that morning, "you have to remember that this was a drunken court. Hamlet comments on the general drunkenness. Even at the end it is drink that kills Hamlet and Claudius and Gertrude. Hamlet is at the centre of this corruption and is infected by it."

His voice seemed quieter, more reflective, as if he was thinking of something else. Once he glanced across to Ralph but said nothing. "I'm sorry," he said at the end of the period, "I meant to return your essays but I didn't finish correcting them." A vein in his forehead throbbed. Ralph knew that he was remembering the voices that had shouted from the depths of the night, and he was wondering why they had been so unfair.

"Something's wrong with old Sniffy," said Pongo at the interval. Ralph couldn't stand the amused contempt the pupils had for his stepfather and the way in which he had to suffer it. After all, he had not chosen him. His stepfather never organized games, there was nothing memorable about him.

When he went home after four, the door was unlocked but he couldn't find his mother. She was neither in the living room nor in the kitchen, which was odd since she usually had their meal ready for them when they returned from the school.

He shouted to her but there was no answer. After a while he knocked on her bedroom door and when there was no response he went in. She was lying flat out on the bed, face down, and was quite still. For a moment his heart leapt with the fear that she might be dead and he turned her over quickly. She was breathing but there was a smell of drink from her. She had never drunk much in her life as far as he knew. There was a bottle of sherry, with a little drink at the bottom of it, beside her on the floor. He slapped her face but she only grunted and didn't waken.

He didn't know what to do. He ran to the bathroom and filled a glass with water and threw it in her face. She shook and coughed while water streamed down her face, then opened her eyes. When she saw him she shut them again.

"Go way," she said in a slurred voice, "Go way."

He stood for a while at the door looking at her. It seemed to him that this was the very end. It had happened because of the events of the previous night. Maybe he should kill himself. Maybe he should hang or drown himself. Or take pills. And then he thought that his mother might have done that. He ran to her bedroom and checked the bottle with the sleeping tablets, but it seemed quite full. He noticed for the first time his own picture on the sideboard opposite the bed where his mother was still sleeping. He picked it up and looked at it: there was no picture of his father there at all.

In the picture he was laughing and his mother was standing just behind him, her right hand resting on his right shoulder. He must have been five or six when the photograph was taken. It astonished him that the photograph should be there at all for he had thought she had forgotten all about him. There was not even a photograph of his stepfather in the room.

And then he heard again the voices coming out of the dark and it was as if he was his stepfather. "Sniffy the Poof, Sniffy the Poof." It was as if he was in that room listening to them. You couldn't be called anything worse than a poof. He heard again his mother telling him about his father. A recollection came back to him of a struggle one night between his mother and father. She had pulled herself away and shouted, "I'm going to take the car and I'm going to kill myself. I know the place where I can do it." And he himself had said to his father, "Did you hear that?" But his father had simply smiled and said, "Your mother's very theatrical." For some reason this had amused him.

She was now sleeping fairly peacefully, sometimes snorting, her hands spread out across the bed.

And his stepfather hadn't come home. Where was he? Had something happened to him? At that moment he felt terror greater than he had ever known, as if he was about to fall down, as if he was spinning in space. What if his mother died, if both of them died, and he was left alone?

He ran to the school as fast as he could. The janitor, who was standing outside his little office with a bunch of keys in his hand, watched him as he crossed the hall, but said nothing.

His stepfather was sitting at his desk on his tall gaunt chair staring across towards the seats. He was still wearing his gown and looked like a ghost inside its holed chalky armour. Even though he must have heard Ralph coming in he didn't turn his head. Ralph had never seen him like this before, so stunned, so helpless. Always, before, his stepfather appeared to have been in control of things. Now he didn't seem to know anything or to be able to do anything. He had wound down.

Ralph stood and looked at him from the doorway. If it weren't for his mother he wouldn't be there.

"Should you not be coming home?" he asked. His stepfather didn't answer. It was as if he was asking a profound question of the desks, as if they had betrayed him. Ralph again felt the floor spinning beneath him. Perhaps it was all too late. Perhaps it was all over. It might be that his stepfather would never come home again, had given everything up. His gaze interrogated the room.

Ralph advanced a little more.

"Should you not be coming home?" he asked again. But still his stepfather retained his pose, a white chalky statue. It was his turn now to be on his own listening to his own questions. Ralph had never thought of him like that before. Always he had been with his mother, always it was he himself who had been the forsaken one. On the blackboard were written the words, "A tragedy gives us a feeling of waste." Ralph stayed where he was for a long time. He didn't know what to do, how to get through to this man whom he had never understood. The empty desks frightened him. The room was like an empty theatre. Once his father had taken him to one in the afternoon. "You wait there," he said, "I have to see someone." And then he had seen his father talking to a girl who was standing face to face with him, wearing a belted raincoat. They had talked earnestly to each other, his father laughing, the girl looking at him adoringly.

No, it could not be true. His father hadn't been at all like that, his father had been the one who adored him, his son. What was this ghost like when compared to his father?

He couldn't bring himself to move, it was as if he was fixed to the floor. There was no word he could think of that would break this silence, this deathly enchantment.

He felt curiously awkward as if his body was something he carried about with him but which was distinct from his mind. It was as if in its heaviness and oddness it belonged to someone else. He thought of his mother outstretched on the bed, her hair floating down her face, stirring in the weak movement of her breath. Something must be done, he couldn't leave this man here and his mother there.

Slowly his stepfather got down from his desk, then placed the jotters which were stacked beside him in a cupboard. Then he locked the cupboard. He had finished marking them after all and would be able to return them. Then he began to walk past Ralph as if he wasn't there, his gaze fixed straight ahead of him. He was walking almost like a mechanical toy, clumsily, his gown fixed about him but becalmed.

Now he was near the door and soon he would be out in the hall. In those seconds, which seemed eternal, Ralph knew that he was facing the disintegration of his whole life. He knew that it was right there, in front of him, if he couldn't think of the magic word. He knew what tragedy was, knew it to its bitter bones, that it was the time that life continued, having gone beyond communication. He knew that tragedy was the thing you couldn't do anything about, that at that point all things are transformed, they enter another dimension, that it is not acting but the very centre of despair itself. He knew it was pitiful, yet the turning point of a life. And in its light, its languageless light, his father's negligent cheerful face burned, the moustache was like straw on fire. He was moving away from him, winking, perhaps deceitful. He saw the burden on this man's shoulders, he saw the desperate loneliness, so like his own. He felt akin to this being who was moving towards the door. And at that moment he found the word and it was as if it had been torn bleeding from his mouth.

"Come on home," he said. "Jim."

Nothing seemed to be happening. Then suddenly the figure came to a halt and stood there at the door as if thinking. It thought like this for a long time. Then it turned to face him. And something in its face seemed to crack as if chalk were cracking and a human face were showing through. Without a word being said the ghost removed its gown and laid it on a desk, then the two of them were walking across the now empty hall towards the main door.

Such a frail beginning, and yet a beginning. Such a small hope, and yet a hope. Almost but not quite side by side, they crossed the playground together and it echoed with their footsteps, shining, too, with a blatant blankness after the rain.

THE RING

IN MY SECONDARY school in those years long ago, when I wore shorts and could feel the wind on my knees, the main romance was that between Mr MacColl (whom we called Frothy) and Miss Simpson. Mr MacColl taught Mathematics and the reason we called him Frothy was that when he got into a rage, which he often used to do because for instance we couldn't understand the (to him) pristine obviousness of Pythagoras' Theorem, he foamed at the mouth so that if you were sitting in the front seat spittle beaded and bubbled on the desk. His face would become a bright red, like a cockerel's, and then after a while white as chalk. Strangely enough, for all his angry outbursts, we rather liked him, for we knew that his rage was not directed at us personally but rather at the abstract beings who had failed to learn that which was so evident to him; but who could however still be saved. And indeed on good days, he would be quite cheerful and even joking, and we would feel protected and secure in his world of triangles and circles and parallelograms. At the same time we thought of him as a comic figure whose trousers were always above his ankles; and sometimes he would say ludicrous things like,

"Watch this blackboard while I go through it again," and we would smile and giggle behind our hands; and I could swear now, looking back, that these clumsinesses were intended, or if not intended, that he himself saw them as being as funny as we did. All in all, we liked him as much as we liked any teacher in the school, though he belted us quite often, for we knew that in his own way he loved us. Yes, I think I could put it as high as that.

Miss Simpson on the other hand I was never taught by, for I didn't take Science, but I remember her as being short, rather squat, and yellow-faced. I have a vague memory that she was also splay-footed.

The romance between the two of them, for they must have been well over forty when I first knew them, had been a source of gossip and merriment in the school for many years, and indeed I had heard even my older brother talking about it. Sometimes a boy or girl would come into Frothy's room with a note: Frothy would study it for a while and then write an answer making sure that it was well sealed. We could tell from his later behaviour whether the note had contained good news or bad. The messenger would smile significantly at us while Frothy was reading the note, and then we knew it had come from Miss Simpson.

I don't know where Frothy stayed (some teachers stayed in the Hostel, but I don't think he was one of them). I think he would have lodged with a landlady in the town: he certainly didn't own a car, or a bicycle, and I think he walked home from school to where his home was.

I myself had a great love for geometry in those days. I adored the inflexible order of the proofs, the fact that parallel lines never met, that triangles were always composed of 180 degrees. One knew where one was with geometry, it was a world of security and happiness, which sprang no surprises, and I always associated it with summer and the warm sun shining on the desk. That such a settled world should exist beyond the tangle and whirl of adolescence was an unexpected gift. It was as if when one had finished a geometry problem one was locking a safe, hearing a satisfactory click.

For this reason I got on well with Frothy, and I liked him though in common with the other boys I considered him eccentric and comic: one could however never admit that one had any feelings at all for a teacher. So there I would sit at my desk in my shorts and Frothy would glance at the proof I had so elegantly created, and find it good. In fact I think I must have entered that world of geometry as a shelter against the difficulties which I had at home at the time, though these are irrelevant to my story. At any rate what I remember best is the safety of those days: Frothy pacing about in his torn gown, the windows bright with light. In a strange way I felt that such days would never come again, and that I owed Frothy their harmony and richness.

There is one thing I forgot to say and that is that during his paroxysms Frothy would cough a lot, his face reddening, and then after the bout of coughing was over, he would pop a pill into his mouth, though none of us knew what this pill was for.

However, one afternoon, he told me to come with him outside the room, and there with great secrecy asked me if I would go on a message for him to the chemist's and get him some Beecham's Powders. It seemed to me odd that a teacher should ask a pupil to do this, it was a confession of bodily weakness that came queerly from a teacher who by definition was a being without illness or frailty. After all, teachers were invincible beings who appeared at the beginning of a period and left at the end of it: in a sense their gowns suggested that they were not human beings at all, like the rest of us. Nor did they ever ask if there was anything wrong with us. The flesh had nothing to do with teaching, one never saw a teacher who was really ill.

However I did go for the powders to the chemist's and all the time I was walking along the street, now and again giving a sudden little skip, I giggled to myself. What a story I would have to tell the others. Frothy sending me for Beecham's Powders. What an extraordinary thing, how essentially funny it was. Nor did it occur to me to wonder why Frothy had sent me rather than anybody else. Had he perhaps thought that I would be different from the other boys and keep my story to myself? If he had thought that he was very much mistaken. And also I took my time on the errand, for I believed like all the other boys that one should never do anything for a teacher with any enthusiasm. I therefore walked slowly down the street, passing the shop where I used to buy *Titbits* and *Answers*. I waited outside the chemist's for a while watching a yacht in the harbour riding up and down on the waves, tethered to its anchor.

When I had got the Beecham's Powders, I put them in my pocket along with the change that I had received from the chemist, who wore a white gown and had an abstracted air like a busy doctor. I didn't have a watch in those days and I kept looking at the clock which was fixed on top of the Town Hall. I wanted to make sure that the period was up before I got back, not because I didn't like geometry, but rather because it was what the boys would have expected of me.

When I got back to the school, the period was over, as I had calculated, and Frothy had left the room. I walked along to the staff-room to find out where he was. All along the corridor the windows were open and the fresh breeze was blowing in. And then I suddenly noticed that at the far end of the corridor, and just outside the staff-room, Frothy and Miss Simpson were standing. I stopped and waited, for I didn't want to intrude on them. As a matter of fact, Frothy's back was turned to me and I could hear him talking in a low passionate voice to Miss Simpson. They were so engaged in their conversation that they didn't notice me. Miss Simpson, like Frothy, was wearing a gown which was white with chalk: she looked like an old splay-footed bat. Frothy's quick speech continued, but Miss Simpson didn't appear to be listening. I couldn't move and pretended to be looking out of one of the windows while at the same time I was thinking that I could gain some information which I would tell the other boys from my class. Their voices were now raised and finally Miss Simpson strode away in the other direction, her gown flying about her. Before she did so she flung something on the stone floor of the corridor, and it rolled along till it came to rest against the wall. I looked down. It was a ring, and it had a red stone in it. It was not unlike those rings that I used to see in Woolworth's when I visited it at the lunch break in order to see if there were any good books I could buy. The sun flashed from the gold of the ring, from its circle.

I went up to Frothy who still had his back to me and said, "Please, sir.'

He turned on me a face bereft of all expression, a totally empty face, and one which was deathly pale.

It was as if he didn't recognize me.

"Please, sir," I said again.

Then it was as if his face assumed expression, became firm and set, knowledge returned to the eyes, and he said,

"Oh, it's you, Turner."

"Yes, sir, please, sir." And I handed him the Beecham's

Powders and he took them and waved away the change which I offered from my sweaty hand. It seemed to me at that moment that he was not like a teacher at all, and that his lips were trembling.

I nearly said to him that the ring was lying on the floor and that if he wanted me to I would retrieve it for him but I didn't say anything. I moved away from him, as from something irretrievably stricken, and ran with the light steps of youth to my next class. I suppose he must have bent down to get the ring, for no one found it later, but I didn't see him doing it.

I was trembling with excitement all through the next class which was Latin, and where I wrote down a long list of irregular verbs. After the period was over I told the others my story. They would hardly believe me, and my news ran through the whole school: the engagement had been broken off. That, I was told, was the significance of the thrown ring. In any case pupils later noticed the abstraction and bad temper of the two protagonists. What a story—a broken romance, a romance that was finally over. And so it proved. They were never seen together again. And never again did Frothy send anyone for Beecham's Powders, as far as I know.

Some hope that he had nourished finally died that day and he became fiercer and fiercer. No, he did not love us any longer, he hated us, he was determined that we would learn about algebra and geometry, not for our own sakes but for his own. The number of passes increased and, as they did so, so we grew to hate him more and more. Then as I climbed the school, shedding my shorts and wearing trousers, I forgot about him, for we now had a different teacher.

Today I opened the paper and read that Frothy had died in an Old People's Home in the town where he had taught. I had heard vague stories about him, that he had become odder and odder, his rages more and more incoherent, the pupils uncontrollable and hostile. No one however dared to be unruly in Miss Simpson's class. I thought of him sitting in a chill breeze outside the Old People's Home, shadows shaped like parallelograms at his feet while his hands trembled under a red blanket. I often wondered what the quarrel had been about but I never found out. I despised myself for the horrid little squirt that I had been and decided to go to his funeral.

It was a fine summer's day again, and there were only a very few people there, not even Miss Simpson, whom I would certainly have recognized even after all those years. I had hoped that there might have been a representation from the school but there wasn't. The only person I met there whom I knew was Soupy who had been in the same class and was now a reporter on the local paper. As the coffin was being lowered into the ground I said to him,

"Tragic, isn't it?"

"Yes," he said. Then he glanced at me in a peculiar way and said, "It was you who found the ring on the floor, wasn't it?"

"Yes," I said.

"That was the day they broke off the engagement. I heard you handed it to him and he burst out crying. He had sent you for a tonic or something, isn't that right?"

"That's not true," I said. "He didn't burst out crying." And I was suddenly angry with Soupy for getting all the facts wrong.

"It doesn't matter," he said catching up with me. "Do you know that he had a stroke the year before he was due to retire. Miss Simpson never went to see him. She's still quite fit, I saw her the other day. She was striding along the front looking like a boxer. She wore tweeds and had a dog with her. Are you coming for a drink?"

"Sorry," I said, "I haven't got time." And I left him.

The chemist's I had bought the Beecham's Powders from was no longer there. In its place was a grocer's shop.

It seemed to me that the best thing about geometry was it never lied to you, which is why I myself am a mathematics teacher as well. It has nothing to do with pain or loss. Its refuge is always secure and without mythology.

GREATER LOVE

HE WORE A ghostly white moustache and looked like a major in the First World War which is exactly what he had been. On our way to school—he being close to retiring age—he would tell me stories about the First World War and the Second World War, for he had been in both. As we were passing the chemist's shop he would be describing Passchendaele, walking along, stiff and erect, his eyes glittering behind his glasses.

"And there I was crouched in this trench, with my water bottle empty. I had somehow or another survived. All my good boys were dead, some of them up to their chests in mud. The Jerries had got hold of our plans of attack, you see. What was I to do? I had to wait till night, that was clear. When the sun was just going down I crawled along the trench and then across No Man's Land. I met a Jerry and the struggle was fast and furious. I am afraid I had to use the bayonet. But the worst was not over yet, for one of my sentries fired on me. But I eventually managed to give him the password. After that I was all right."

He would pause and then as we passed the ironmonger's he would start on another story. He taught Chemistry in the school and instead of telling his pupils about solutions or whatever they do in Chemistry, he would spend his time talking about the Marne or the Somme. He spoke more about the First World War than about the Second.

Once at a school party there was a quarrel between him and the Head of the English Department, who also had been in the First World War and believed that he had won it. He questioned a statement which Morrison had made. It was, I think, a question of a date, and they grew more and more angry, and wouldn't speak to each other after that for a year or more. As I quite liked both of them, it was difficult to know whose side to take.

The headmaster didn't know what to do with him, for parents came to the school continually to complain about his lessons, which as I have said consisted mostly of accounts of his

adventures in France and Flanders. The extraordinary thing
was that he never repeated a story: all his tales were realistic and
detailed and one could almost believe that they had happened.
Either these things had been experienced by him or they formed
part of a huge mythology of legends which he had memorized,
but that had happened to others. I was then Deputy Head of the
school and it was my duty to see the parents and listen to their
complaints.

"He will soon be retiring," I would tell them soothingly, "and
he has been a good teacher in his time." And they would answer,
"That's all very well but our children's education is being
ruined. When are you going to speak to him?" I did in fact try to
speak to him a few times but before I could start he was telling
me another of his stories and I found, somehow or another, that
there was no way in which I could introduce my complaint to
him.

"There was an angel, you know, at Mons and I saw it. It was
early morning and we were going over the top and we saw this
figure with white wings bending over us from the sky. I thought
it must have been an effect of the sun but it wasn't that. It was as
if it was blessing us. We had our bayonets out and the light was
flashing from them. I was in charge of a company at the time, the
Colonel—Colonel Wilson—having been killed."

This time I was so interested that I said to him, "Are you quite
sure that it was an angel? After all the rays of the sun streaming
down, and you I presume being in an excited frame of
mind . . .?"

"No," he said, "it wasn't that. It was definitely an angel. I am
quite sure of that. I could actually see its eyes." And he turned to
me. "They were so compassionate, you have no idea what they
looked like. You could never forget them."

In those days we had lines and the pupils would assemble in
the quadrangle in front of the main door, and Morrison loved
the little military drill so much that we gave him the duty most
of the time. He would make them dress, keeping two paces
between the files, and they would march into the school in an
orderly manner.

A young bearded teacher called Cummings, who was always bringing educational books into the staff-room, didn't like this militarism at all. One day he said to me, "He's teaching them to be soldiers. He should be stopped."

"How old are you?" I asked him.

"Twenty-two. What's that to do with it?"

"Twenty-two," I said. "Run along and teach your pupils French."

He didn't like it but I didn't want to explain to him why his age was so important. Still, I couldn't find a way of speaking to Morrison without offending him.

"You'll just have to come straight out with it," my wife said.

"No," I said.

"What else can you do?"

"I don't know," I said.

I was very conscious of the fact that I was fifteen years younger than Morrison.

One day I said to him, "How do you see your pupils?"

"What do you mean?" he asked.

"How do you see them?" I repeated.

"See them?" he said. And then, "They are too young to fight, yet, but I see them as ready for it. Soon they will be taken."

"Taken?"

"Yes," he said. "Just as we were taken."

After a silence he said, "One or two of them would make good officers. It's the gas that's the worst."

"Have you told them about the gas?" I said, seizing on a tenuous connection between the First World War and Chemistry.

"No," he said, "it was horrifying."

"Well," I said, "explain to them about the gas. Why don't you do that?"

"We never used it," he said. "The Jerries tried to use it but the wind was against them." However he promised that he would explain about the gas. I was happy that I had found a method of getting him to teach something of his subject and tried to think of other connections. But I couldn't think of any more.

One day he came to see me and said, "A parent called on me today."

"Called on you?" I said angrily. "He should have come through me."

"I know," he said. "He came directly to me. He complained that I was an inefficient teacher. Do you think I'm an inefficient teacher?"

"No," I said.

"I have to warn them, you see," he said earnestly. "But I suppose I had better teach them Chemistry after all."

From that time onwards, he became more and more melancholy and lost-looking. He drifted through the corridors with his white ghostly moustache, as if he was looking for a battle to take part in. Then he stopped coming to the staff-room and stayed in his classroom all the time. There were another three months to go to his retirement and if he carried on this way I knew that he would fade away and die. Parents ceased to come and see me about him, but I was worried.

One day I called the best Chemistry student in the school—Harrison—to my room and I said,

"How is Mr Morrison these days?"

Harrison paused a moment,

"He's very absent minded, sir," he said at last. We looked at each other meaningfully, he tall and handsome in his blue uniform with the gold braid at the cuffs of his jacket. I fancied for a terrible moment that I saw a ghostly white moustache flowering at his lips.

"I see," I said, fiddling with a pen which was lying on top of the red blotting paper which in turn was stained with drops of ink, like flak.

"How are you managing, the members of the class, I mean?" I said.

"We'll be all right, sir," said Harrison. Though nothing had been said between us he knew what I was talking about.

"I'll leave you to deal with it, then," I said.

The following day Morrison came gleefully to see me.

"An extraordinary thing happened to me," he said. "Do you

know that boy Harrison? He is very brilliant of course and will
certainly go to University. He asked me about the First World
War. He was very interested. I think he will make a good
officer."

"Oh," I said.

"He has a very fine mind. His questions were very searching."

"I see," I said, doodling furiously.

"I cannot disguise the fact that I was unhappy there for a
while. I was thinking, 'Here they are and I am not able to warn
them of what is going to happen to them.' You see, no one told us
then there would be two World Wars. I was in Sixth year when
the First World War broke out and I was studying Chemistry
just like Harrison. They told us that we would be home for
Christmas. Then after I came back from the war I did Chemistry
in University. I forgot about the war, and then the Second one
came along. By that time I was teaching here, as you know."

"Yes," I said.

"In the First World War everyone was so young. We were so
ignorant. No one told us anything. We were very enthusiastic,
you see. You recollect of course that there hadn't been a really
big war since the Napoleonic War. Of course there had been the
Boer War and the Crimean War but these were side issues."

"Of course," I said.

"You were in the Second World War yourself," he said, "so
you will know."

But as I had been in the Air Force that didn't in his opinion
count. And yet I too had seen scarves of flame like those of
students streaming from 'planes as they exploded in the sky. I felt
the responsibility of my job intensely. Though I was so much
younger I felt as if I was the older of the two. I felt protective
towards him as if it was I who was the officer and he the young
starry-eyed recruit.

After Harrison had asked him his questions Morrison was
quite happy again and could return to the First World War with
a clear conscience. Then one day a parent came to see me. It was
in fact Major Beith, a red faced man with a fierce moustache
who had been an officer in the Second World War.

"What the bloody hell is going on?" he asked me. "My son isn't learning any Chemistry. Have you seen his report card? It's bloody awful."

"He doesn't work," I said firmly.

"I'm not saying that he's the best worker in the world. The bugger watches TV all the time but that's not the whole explanation. He's not being taught. He got fifteen per cent for his Chemistry."

I was silent for a while and then I said,

"Education is a very strange thing."

"What?" And he glared at me from below his bushy eyebrows.

I leaned towards him and said, "What do you think education consists of?"

"Consists of? I send my son to this school to be taught. That's what education consists of. But the little bugger tells me that all he learns about is the Battle of the Marne."

"Yes," I said, "I appreciate that. But on the other hand I sometimes think that . . ." I paused. "He sees them, I don't know how he sees them. He sees them as the Flowers of Flanders. Can you believe that?"

His bulbous eyes raked me as if with machine-gun fire.

"I don't know what you're talking about."

I sighed. "Perhaps not. He sees them as potential officers and NCO's and privates. He is trying to warn them. He is trying to tell them what it was like. He loves them, you see."

"Loves them?"

"That's right. He is their commanding officer. He is preparing them." And then I said, daringly, "What's Chemistry in comparison with that."

He looked at me in amazement. "Do you know," he said, "that I am on the education committee?"

"Yes," I said, staring him full in the eye.

"And you're supposed to be in charge of discipline here."

"I am," I said. "I have to think of everything. Teachers have rights too."

"What do you mean teachers have rights?"

"Exactly what I said. If pupils have rights so have teachers. And one cannot legislate for love. He loves them more than you or I are capable of loving. He sees the horror awaiting them. To him Chemistry is irrelevant."

For the first time I saw a gleam of understanding passing across the cloudless sky of his eyes. About to get up, he sat down again, smoothing his kilt.

"It's an unusual situation," I said. "And by the nature of things it will not last long. The fact is that we don't know the horrors in that man's mind. Every day he is in there he sees his class being charged with bayonets. He sees Germans in grey helmets. He smells the gas seeping into the room. He is protecting them. All he has is his stories to save them."

"You think?" he said looking at me shrewdly.

"I do," I said.

"I see," he said, in his crisp military manner.

"He is not like us," I said. "He is being destroyed by his imagination." As a matter of fact I knew that his son was lazy and difficult and that part of the reason for that was the affair the major was carrying on with a married woman from the same village.

He thought for a while and then he said, "He has only two or three months to go, I suppose. We can last it out."

"I knew you would understand," I said.

He shook his head in a puzzled manner and then left the room.

The day before he was due to retire Morrison came to see me.

"They are as prepared as I can make them," he said. "There is nothing more I can do for them."

"You've done very well," I said.

"I have tried my best," he said.

"Question and answer," he said. "I should have done it in that way, but they didn't know enough. One should start from the known and work out towards the unknown. But they didn't know enough so I had to start with the unknown."

"There was no other way," I said.

"Thank you," he said courteously. And he leaned across the desk and shook me by the hand.

I said that I hoped he would enjoy his retirement but he didn't answer.

"Goodbye for the present," I said. "I'm afraid I shall have to be away tomorrow. A meeting, you understand."

His eyes clouded over for a moment and then he said,

"Well, goodbye then."

"Goodbye," I said. I thought for one terrible moment that he would salute but he didn't.

As a matter of fact I didn't see him often after his retirement. It was time that Chemistry was taught properly. Later however I heard that he had lost his memory and couldn't tell his stories of the World War any more.

I felt this as an icy bouquet on my tongue. But the slate had to be cleaned, education had to begin again.

THE SNOWBALLS

"THE MINISTER, THE Reverend Murdo Mackenzie, and his son, Kenneth, will be visiting the school tomorrow," Mr Macrae told the boys of Standard Seven. "I want you to be on your best behaviour." They sat two to a seat in a room which was white with the light of the snow.

"That is all I have to say about it," he said. He unfurled a map which he stretched across the blackboard. "And now," he said, "we will do some geography."

The following day was again a dazzle of white. Mr Macrae took a watch from his breast pocket and said, "They will be here at eleven o'clock. It is now five to eleven and time for your interval." They rushed out into the playground and immediately began to throw snowballs at each other. They would perhaps have a longer interval today and then Mr Macrae would blow his whistle and they would form lines and march into the room.

Torquil shook his head as he received a snowball in the face and then ran after Daial, whom he hit with a beauty. The sky was clear and blue, and the snow crisp and fresh and white.

At eleven o'clock they saw a stout sombre man clad in black climb the icy steps to the playground, a small pale boy beside him. They stopped throwing snowballs for they knew this was the minister. He halted solidly in the middle of the playground and said,

"This is my son Kenneth. I shall leave him with you for a while. I am going to see Mr Macrae." He had a big red face and a white collar which cut into his thick red neck. Mr Macrae was waiting for him at the door and they saw him bend forward a little as he welcomed the minister into the school.

"Come on," said Torquil to the small pale Kenneth. "You can join in if you want." Kenneth seemed at first not to know what to do, and he stood uncertainly in the middle of the playground, while all around him the boys whirled and shouted and threw snowballs. Then he too began to throw snowballs and after a while he was enjoying himself hugely, and his pale face glowed with colour. He got a snowball in the back of the neck but he gave another one back, though he slipped once or twice being not at all sure on his feet. He ran almost like a girl with his hands in front of him. The interval passed quickly and then just at the moment that Kenneth had received another snowball, this time on the cheek, Mr Macrae and the minister appeared at the door.

They saw the minister stride wrathfully forward after saying something to Mr Macrae and still with the same uninterrupted stride descend the icy steps, his hand in his son's hand, and disappear from view. Mr Macrae blew his whistle and they all lined up, still red and panting from their exertions. As they stood in line they saw that Mr Macrae was trembling with rage and his face was white.

His moustache bristled as he shouted,

"So you threw snowballs at the minister's son, eh? Eh? I will teach you." While they still waited in line he went furiously back into the school-room and emerged with a belt. "So that you will know what you are being belted for," he said, "you are getting it for throwing snowballs at the minister's son. You have made me a laughing stock. The minister's son is at a private school and is not used to such behaviour. You have shown yourselves to be hooligans, that's what you have done."

"Hold out your hand," he said to Daial, who was at the head of the line. They heard the belt whistle through the air six times. "Now your other hand," said Mr Macrae. Torquil waited. He was sixth in line. He knew that the belt would be very sore on such a cold winter's day. He spat on his two hands in preparation. Swish went the belt and the more he belted the more fierce became Mr Macrae's rage.

While he was waiting to be belted Torquil said to himself, "Kenneth was enjoying the snowballing. Why are we being belted?" But he knew that the belting didn't have anything to do with Kenneth, it had to do with the minister, and perhaps not even with the minister but with Mr Macrae. Deep within himself he felt the unfairness of it: twelve of the belt for throwing snowballs, that was not right. Ahead of him he heard the Mouse

whimpering quietly and saw him bending down, wringing his
hands as if he were in unbearable pain. Mr Macrae now reached
him and said, "Hold out your hand, boy," not "Torquil" but
"boy." He did so and the first stroke had a sting that made him
wince. The second one was worse and by the time that the sixth
one came he felt that his hand had been cut. He gritted his teeth
as tightly as he could. "The other hand," said Mr Macrae, his
small pale moustached face fierce and determined. The belt rose
and fell, rose and fell. For one crazy moment Torquil thought of
withdrawing his hand and then decided against it, even though
he was as tall as Mr Macrae if it came to a struggle. Then it was
all over and they were back in the classroom again.

They sat down in their seats and for a while Mr Macrae
turned his back on the class, breathing heavily as if still not
satiated.

Many of the boys were wringing their hands under the desks
and the Mouse was still whimpering quietly.

"That's enough," said Mr Macrae and the Mouse stopped
whimpering.

The boys opened their poetry books and they read round the
class.

> "A wet sheet and a flowing sea
>   a wind that follows fast
> and fills the white and rustling sail
>   and bends the gallant mast
> and bends the gallant mast, my boys,
>   while like the eagle free
> away the good ship flies and leaves
>   old England on the lee."

Mr Macrae beat with his ruler on the desk as if it was a
metronome.

> "There's témpest in yon hórned móon,
>   and líghtning in yon clóud
> But hárk the músic máriners
>   the wínd is píping lóud."

Suddenly he seemed to have become jolly again and to have forgotten the belting and the snowballing.

> "The wínd is píping lóud, my bóys,
>   the líghtning fláshes frée,
> while the hóllow óak our pálace ís,
>   our héritage the séa,

Torquil put his hand up.
"What is it, Campbell?"
"Please, sir, I want to go to the toilet."

"All right then, all right then," said Mr Macrae in the same jolly voice. Torquil left the room and went outside into the whiteness. It was snowing gently and the flakes broke like stars on his jacket and his white trousers. The toilet at the back of the school was cold and draughty, and there was no lock on the door. The water poured down the walls. He stood there for a while contemplatively peeing, his hands so raw and red that he had difficulty in unfastening and then fastening his fly.

After a while he left the toilet and went into the school again. As he was coming in the door he saw Mr Macrae standing there, while from the classroom whose door was shut he could hear the boys chanting in unison,

> "O for a sóft and géntle bréeze
>   I héard the fáir one crý
> but gíve to me the snóring bréeze
>   and white waves héaving hígh."

"And white waves heaving high," said Mr Macrae jocularly. "So you will throw snowballs at the minister's son." And he made to hit Torquil on the bottom with the belt, but Torquil slid away and was hit on the head instead. For a moment a phantom fighter turned on Mr Macrae and then he was back in the classroom again, sitting in his seat. Mr Macrae was now in a good mood and shouting,

"And bends the gallant mast, my boys. Can't you see it, boys, the ship with all sails set crowding across the ocean. The storm can do nothing to her for as we are told in the poem the good ship was tight and free. What is the hollow oak, Torquil?" Torquil looked up at him out of the gathering swaying darkness into which he abruptly fell, the ocean closing over him.

"Torquil," shouted the headmaster and then there was complete darkness. Later he felt himself being set on his feet. Cold water was streaming down his face. Mr Macrae was speaking to him nervously.

"Are you all right, Torquil?"

"Yes, sir."

"Good, good. You can go home then. Did you hear me? You may go home. Tell your father I shall be along later." Torquil stood on the floor, no longer swaying.

"Fine, fine," said Mr Macrae, "it was an accident, you understand."

Torquil left the classroom and walked across the playground and down the steps and then turned left to go home. The snow was still falling, very lightly, on his jacket. Soon it would be Christmas, he thought.

When he went in the door his mother looked up. Her hands were white with flour.

"I'm not going back," said Torquil.

"What did you say?"

"I'm not going back. Ever," said Torquil.

"I am going for your father," said his mother, and she went into the byre where her husband was busy with harness.

"Torquil has come home," she said, "and says he's not going back to school again."

Her husband raised his grave pale bearded face and said,

"I will see him. Tell him to come in here."

She went back into the house and told Torquil,

"Your father wants to see you in the byre."

Torquil went into the byre where his father was waiting. The smell of leather calmed him: he would like to learn how to plough. Next spring he would ask his father to let him.

"What is all this?" said his father. "Sit on that chest." Torquil sat down.

"Well, then," said his father.

Torquil told him his story. He tried to tell his father that the worst part of it was not the belting but the difference between him and the minister's son, but he couldn't put into words what he felt. He put his raw hands under his bottom as he sat on the chest. His father didn't say anything for a long while and then he said,

"Mr Macrae is a good man. He is a good teacher."

"Yes, father," said Torquil.

"The one before him was too slack." Then he stopped. "I will think about it." Then, "Mr Macrae is a good Navigation teacher," he added as if this was as important. "Go inside now."

At half past four Torquil saw Mr Macrae heading for the house on his bicycle, a small figure on which the snow was falling. Through the window, itself almost covered with snow, he saw him approaching and then his father going to meet him. He couldn't hear what Mr Macrae was saying but saw that he was gesticulating. His father stared at the ground and then shook his head. He seemed to be much calmer than Mr Macrae who was like a wasp humming about a bull. Then after Mr Macrae had talked a great deal, Torquil saw him get on his bike and ride away. After he had gone his father sent for him.

"You are not going back to school," he said. "You will work with me on the croft. We will say no more about it."

Torquil saw that his mother was about to say something but his father looked at her and she bent her head to the plate again.

That spring Torquil was allowed to help his father with the ploughing which was harder than he had thought. The plough refused to go in a straight line, the patient horse tugged and tugged. Seagulls flew about the sparse ground, and a fresh wind was in his nostrils. Sometimes as he walked along he could hear a voice in his head saying

> And bends the gallant mast, my boys,
>   while like the eagle free
> away the good ship flies and leaves
>   old England on the lee.

The black earth turned and the blades were hit by stones. He felt as if he was captain of a ship, his jersey billowing in the breeze.

"You'll come on fine," said his father and then to his mother that night. "He's coming along fine."

When he was eighteen years old, because there was no employment, he decided to emigrate to Canada. He stood on the pier, his father and mother beside him. The ship's sails swelled in the breeze.

"You will be all right," said his father. "You have a good grounding in Navigation. Mr Macrae saw to that."

"Yes," Torquil agreed.

He went on board the ship after kissing his mother and shaking his father by the hand. As the ship sailed away from the pier he saw them standing there with a lot of other people who were seeing relatives off. The sails swelled and soon they were far from shore and the island was a long line of green with lights twinkling here and there. Then it could not be seen at all.

He had a hard time of it in Canada for it was during the thirties that he emigrated. Sometimes he slept in doss-houses, sometimes he worked on the railway tracks. At nights he and the other boys from Scotland kept themselves warm by dancing the Highland Fling. His underclothes were in rags and one morning in spring after washing them in a stream he threw them away. Eventually he reached Vancouver and there got a job as a Fire Officer. He trained hoses on charred bodies in burnt rooms.

One night at a ceilidh in another islander's house he had an argument with him about the Garden of Eden.

"It wasn't an apple that was mentioned," he said. "It was just any fruit. I'll show you." And, after asking him to get his Bible, they both studied it. It didn't mention an apple at all. It simply said the Tree of Good and Evil.

"You know your Bible sure enough," said the islander whose name was Smith, and who was lame because of an accident on the grain elevators.

Torquil didn't say anything.

"The funny thing is that I never see you in church," said Smith.

"You will never see me in church," said Torquil.

But he didn't say why not. It seemed to him strange that he felt no anger towards Macrae whom he still regarded as having been a good teacher, especially of Navigation. Sometimes when it was snowing gently he would see the belt descending, he could hear the words of that poem which he had never forgotten and he could see the thick neck and face of the minister.

"No," he repeated, "You'll never see me there."

THE PLAY

WHEN HE STARTED teaching first Mark Mason was very enthusiastic, thinking that he could bring to the pupils gifts of the poetry of Wordsworth, Shakespeare and Keats. But it wasn't going to be like that, at least not with Class 3g. 3g was a class of girls who, before the raising of the school leaving age, were to leave at the end of their fifteenth year. Mark brought them "relevant" poems and novels including *Timothy Winters* and *Jane Eyre* but quickly discovered that they had a fixed antipathy to the written word. It was not that they were undisciplined— that is to say they were not actively mischievous—but they were thrawn: he felt that there was a solid wall between himself and them and that no matter how hard he sold them *Jane Eyre*, by reading chapters of it aloud, and comparing for instance the food in the school refectory that Jane Eyre had to eat with that which they themselves got in their school canteen, they were not interested. Indeed one day when he was walking down one of the aisles between two rows of desks he asked one of the girls, whose name was Lorna and who was pasty-faced and blond, what was the last book she had read, and she replied,

"Please, sir, I never read any books."

This answer amazed him for he could not conceive of a world where one never read any books and he was the more determined to introduce them to the activity which had given himself so much pleasure. But the more enthusiastic he became, the more eloquent his words, the more they withdrew into themselves till finally he had to admit that he was completely failing with the class. As he was very conscientious this troubled him, and not even his success with the academic classes compensated for his obvious lack of success with this particular class. He believed in any event that failure with the non-academic classes constituted failure as a teacher. He tried to do creative writing with them first by bringing in reproductions of paintings by Magritte which were intended to awaken in their minds a glimmer of the unexpectedness and strangeness of ordinary things, but they would simply look at them and point out to him their lack of resemblance to reality. He was in despair. His failure began to obsess him so much that he discussed the problem with the Head of Department who happened to be teaching *Rasselas* to the Sixth Form at the time with what success Mark could not gauge.

"I suggest you make them do the work," said his Head of Department. "There comes a point where if you do not impose your personality they will take advantage of you."

But somehow or another Mark could not impose his personality on them: they had a habit for instance of forcing him to deviate from the text he was studying with them by mentioning something that had appeared in the newspaper.

"Sir," they would say, "did you see in the papers that there were two babies born from two wombs in the one woman." Mark would flush angrily and say, "I don't see what this has to do with our work," but before he knew where he was he was in the middle of an animated discussion which was proceeding all around him about the anatomical significance of this piece of news. The fact was that he did not know how to deal with them: if they had been boys he might have threatened them with the last sanction of the belt, or at least frightened them in some way. But girls were different, one couldn't belt girls, and certainly he couldn't frighten this particular lot. They all wanted to be hairdressers: and one wanted to be an engineer having read in a paper that this was now a possible job for girls. He couldn't find it in his heart to tell her that it was highly unlikely that she could do this without Highers. They fantasized a great deal about jobs and chose ones which were well beyond their scope. It seemed to him that his years in Training College hadn't prepared him for this varied apathy and animated gossip. Sometimes one or two of them were absent and when he asked where they were was told that they were baby sitting. He dreaded the periods he had to try and teach them in, for as the year passed and autumn darkened into winter he knew that he had not taught them anything and he could not bear it.

He talked to other teachers about them, and the History man

shrugged his shoulders and said that he gave them pictures to look at, for instance one showing women at the munitions during the First World War. It became clear to him that their other teachers had written them off since they would be leaving at the end of the session, anyway, and as long as they were quiet they were allowed to talk and now and again glance at the books with which they had been provided.

But Mark, whose first year this was, felt weighed down by his failure and would not admit to it. There must be something he could do with them, the failure was his fault and not theirs. Like a missionary he had come to them bearing gifts, but they refused them, turning away from them with total lack of interest. Keats, Shakespeare, even the ballads, shrivelled in front of his eyes. It was, curiously enough, Mr Morrison who gave him his most helpful advice. Mr Morrison spent most of his time making sure that his register was immaculate, first writing in the O's in pencil and then rubbing them out and re-writing them in ink. Mark had been told that during the Second World War while Hitler was advancing into France, Africa and Russia he had been insisting that his register was faultlessly kept and the names written in carefully. Morrison understood the importance of this though no one else did.

"What you have to do with them," said Morrison, looking at Mark through his round glasses which were like the twin barrels of a gun, "is to find out what they want to do."

"But," said Mark in astonishment, "that would be abdicating responsibility."

"That's right," said Morrison equably.

"If that were carried to its conclusion," said Mark, but before he could finish the sentence Morrison said,

"In teaching nothing ought to be carried to its logical conclusion."

"I see," said Mark, who didn't. But at least Morrison had introduced a new idea into his mind which was at the time entirely empty.

"I see," he said again. But he was not yet ready to go as far as Morrison had implied that he should. The following day however he asked the class for the words of 'Paper Roses', one of the few pop songs that he had ever heard of. For the first time he saw a glimmer of interest in their eyes, for the first time they were actually using pens. In a short while they had given him the words from memory. Then he took out a book of Burns' poems and copied on to the board the verses of 'My Love is Like a Red Red Rose'. He asked them to compare the two poems but found that the wall of apathy had descended again and that it was as impenetrable as before. Not completely daunted, he asked them if they would bring in a record of 'Paper Roses', and himself found one of 'My Love is Like a Red Red Rose', with Kenneth Mackellar singing it. He played both songs, one after the other, on his own record player. They were happy listening to 'Paper Roses' but showed no interest in the other song. The discussion he had planned petered out, except that the following day a small girl with black hair and a pale face brought in a huge pile of records which she requested that he play and which he adamantly refused to do. It occurred to him that the girls simply did not have the ability to handle discussion, that in all cases where discussion was initiated it degenerated rapidly into gossip or vituperation or argument, that the concept of reason was alien to them, that in fact the long line of philosophers beginning with Plato was irrelevant to them. For a long time they brought in records now that they knew he had a record player but he refused to play any of them. Hadn't he gone far enough by playing 'Paper Roses'? No, he was damned if he would go the whole hog and surrender completely. And yet, he sensed that somewhere in this area of their interest was what he wanted, that from here he might find the lever which would move their world.

He noticed that their leader was a girl called Tracy, a fairly tall pleasant-looking girl to whom they all seemed to turn for response or rejection. Nor was this girl stupid: nor were any of them stupid. He knew that he must hang on to that, he must not believe that they were stupid. When they did come into the room it was as if they were searching for substance, a food which he could not provide. He began to study Tracy more and more as if she might perhaps give him the solution to his problem, but she did not appear interested enough to do so. Now and again she would hum the words of a song while engaged in combing another girl's hair, an activity which would satisfy them for hours, and indeed some of the girls had said to him, "Tracy has a good voice, sir. She can sing any pop song you like." And Tracy had regarded him with the sublime self-confidence of one who indeed could do this. But what use would that be to him? More and more he felt himself, as it were, sliding into their world when what he had wanted was to drag them out of the darkness into his world. That was how he himself had been taught and that was how it should be. And the weeks passed and he had taught them nothing. Their jotters were blank apart from the words of pop songs and certain secret drawings of their own. Yet they were human beings, they were not stupid. That there was no such thing as stupidity was the faith by which he lived. In many ways they were quicker than he was, they found out more swiftly than he did the dates of examinations and holidays. They were quite reconciled to the fact that they would not be able to pass any examinations. They would say,

"We're the stupid ones, sir." And yet he would not allow them that easy option, the fault was not with them, it was with him. He had seen some of them serving in shops, in restaurants, and they were neatly dressed, good with money and polite. Indeed they seemed to like him, and that made matters worse for he felt that he did not deserve their liking. They are not fed, he quoted to himself from *Lycidas*, as he watched them at the checkout desks of supermarkets flashing a smile at him, placing the messages in bags much more expertly than he would have done. And indeed he felt that a question was being asked of him but not at all pressingly. At night he would read Shakespeare and think, "There are some people to whom all this is closed. There are some who will never shiver as they read the lines

> Absent thee from felicity awhile
> and in this harsh world draw thy breath in pain
> to tell my story.

If he had read those lines to them they would have thought that
it was Hamlet saying farewell to a girl called Felicity, he thought
wryly. He smiled for the first time in weeks. Am I taking this too
seriously, he asked himself. They are not taking it seriously.
Shakespeare is not necessary for hairdressing. As they endlessly
combed each other's hair he thought of the ballad of Sir Patrick
Spens and the line

<blockquote>wi gowd kaims in their hair.</blockquote>

These girls were entirely sensuous, words were closed to them.
They would look after babies with tenderness but they were not
interested in the alien world of language.

Or was he being a male chauvinist pig? No, he had tried
everything he could think of and he had still failed. The fact was
that language, the written word, was their enemy, McLuhan
was right after all. The day of the record player and television
had transformed the secure academic world in which he had
been brought up. And yet he did not wish to surrender, to get on
with correction while they sat talking quietly to each other, and
dreamed of the jobs which were in fact shut against them. School
was simply irrelevant to them, they did not even protest, they
withdrew from it gently and without fuss. They had looked at
education and turned away from it. It was their indifferent
gentleness that bothered him more than anything. But they also
had the maturity to distinguish between himself and education,
which was a large thing to do. They recognized that he had a job
to do, that he wasn't at all unlikeable and was in fact a prisoner
like themselves. But they were already perming some woman's
hair in a luxurious shop.

The more he pondered, the more he realized that they were
the key to his failure or success in education. If he failed with
them then he had failed totally, a permanent mark would be left
on his psyche. In some way it was necessary for him to change,
but the point was, could he change to the extent that was
demanded of him, and in what direction and with what purpose
should he change? School for himself had been a discipline and

an order but to them this discipline and order had become meaningless.

The words on the blackboard were ghostly and distant as if they belonged to another age, another universe. He recalled what Morrison had said, "You must find out what they want to do", but they themselves did not know what they wanted to do, it was for him to tell them that, and till he told them that they would remain indifferent and apathetic. Sometimes he sensed that they themselves were growing tired of their lives, that they wished to prove themselves but didn't know how to set about it. They were like lost children, irrelevantly stored in desks, and they only lighted up like street lamps in the evening or when they were working in the shops. He felt that they were the living dead, and he would have given anything to see their eyes become illuminated, become interested, for if he could find the magic formula he knew that they would become enthusiastic, they were *not* stupid. But how to find the magic key which would release the sleeping beauties from their sleep? He had no idea what it was and felt that in the end if he ever discovered it he would stumble over it and not be led to it by reflection or logic. And that was exactly what happened.

One morning he happened to be late coming into the room and there was Tracy swanning about in front of the class, as if she were wearing a gown, and saying some words to them he guessed in imitation of himself, while at the same time uncannily reproducing his mannerisms, leaning for instance despairingly across his desk, his chin on his hand while at the same time glaring helplessly at the class. It was like seeing himself slightly distorted in water, slightly comic, frustrated and yet angrily determined. When he opened the door there was a quick scurry and the class had arranged themselves, presenting blank dull faces as before. He pretended he had seen nothing, but knew now what he had to do. The solution had come to him as a gift from heaven, from the gods themselves, and the class sensed a new confidence and purposefulness in his voice.

"Tracy," he said, "and Lorna." He paused. "And Helen. I want you to come out here."

They came out to the floor looking at him uneasily. O my wooden O, he said to himself, my draughty echo help me now.

"Listen," he said, "I've been thinking. It's quite clear to me that you don't want to do any writing, so we won't do any writing. But I'll tell you what we're going to do instead. We're going to act."

A ripple of noise ran through the class, like the wind on an autumn day, and he saw their faces brightening. The shades of Shakespeare and Sophocles forgive me for what I am to do, he prayed.

"We are going," he said, "to do a serial and it's going to be called 'The Rise of a Pop Star'." It was as if animation had returned to their blank dull faces, he could see life sparkling in their eyes, he could see interest in the way they turned to look at each other, he could hear it in the stir of movement that enlivened the room.

"Tracy," he said, "you will be the pop star. You are coming home from school to your parents' house. I'm afraid," he added, "that as in the reverse of the days of Shakespeare the men's parts will have be to be acted by the girls. Tracy, you have decided to leave home. Your parents of course disapprove. But you want to be a pop star, you have always wanted to be one. They think that that is a ridiculous idea. Lorna, you will be the mother, and Helen, you will be the father."

He was astonished by the manner in which Tracy took over, by the ingenuity with which she and the other two created the first scene in front of his eyes. The scene grew and became meaningful, all their frustrated enthusiasm was poured into it.

First of all without any prompting Tracy got her school bag and rushed into the house while Lorna, the mother, pretended to be ironing on a desk that was quickly dragged out into the middle of the floor, and Helen the father read the paper, which was his own *Manchester Guardian* snatched from the top of his desk.

"Well, that's it over," said Tracy, the future pop star.

"And what are you thinking of doing with yourself now?" said the mother, pausing from her ironing.

"I'm going to be a pop star," said Tracy.

"What's that you said?"—her father, laying down the paper.

"That's what I want to do," said Tracy, "other people have done it."

"What nonsense," said the father. "I thought you were going in for hairdressing."

"I've changed my mind," said Tracy.

"You won't stay in this house if you're going to be a pop star," said the father. "I'll tell you that for free."

"I don't care whether I do or not," said Tracy.

"And how are you going to be a pop star?" said her mother.

"I'll go to London," said Tracy.

"London. And where are you going to get your fare from?" said the father, mockingly, picking up the paper again.

Mark could see that Tracy was thinking this over: it was a real objection. Where was her fare going to come from? She paused, her mind grappling with the problem.

"I'll sell my records," she said at last.

Her father burst out laughing. "You're the first one who starts out as a pop star by selling all your records." And then in a sudden rage in which Mark could hear echoes of reality he shouted,

"All right then. Bloody well go then."

Helen glanced at Mark, but his expression remained benevolent and unchanged.

Tracy, turning at the door, said, "Well then, I'm going. And I'm taking the records with me." She suddenly seemed very thin and pale and scrawny.

"Go on then," said her father.

"That's what I'm doing. I'm going." Her mother glanced from daughter to father and then back again but said nothing.

"I'm going then," said Tracy, pretending to go to another room and then taking the phantom records in her arms. The father's face was fixed and determined and then Tracy looked at the two of them for the last time and left the room. The father and mother were left alone.

"She'll come back soon enough," said the father but the mother still remained silent. Now and again the father would look at a phantom clock on a phantom mantelpiece but still Tracy did not return. The father pretended to go and lock a door and then said to his wife,

"I think we'd better go to bed."

And then Lorna and Helen went back to their seats while Mark thought, this was exactly how dramas began in their bareness and naivety, through which at the same time an innocent genuine feeling coursed or peered as between ragged curtains.

When the bell rang after the first scene was over he found himself thinking about Tracy wandering the streets of London, as if she were a real waif sheltering in transient doss-houses or under bridges dripping with rain. The girls became real to him in their rôles whereas they had not been real before, nor even individualistic behind their wall of apathy. That day in the staff-room he heard about Tracy's saga and was proud and non-committal.

The next day the story continued. Tracy paced up and down the bare boards of the classroom, now and again stopping to look at ghostly billboards, advertisements. The girls had clearly been considering the next development during the interval they had been away from him, and had decided on the direction of the plot. The next scene was in fact an Attempted Seduction Scene.

Tracy was sitting disconsolately at a desk which he presumed was a table in what he presumed was a café.

"Hello, Mark," she said to the man who came over to sit beside her. At this point Tracy glanced wickedly at the real Mark. The Mark in the play was the dark-haired girl who had asked for the records and whose name was Annie.

"Hello," said Annie. And then, "I could get you a spot, you know."

"What do you mean?"

"There's a night club where they have a singer and she's sick. I could get you to take her place." He put his hands on hers and she quickly withdrew her own.

"I mean it," he said. "If you come to my place I can introduce you to the man who owns the night club."

Tracy searched his face with forlorn longing.

Was this another lie like the many she had experienced before? Should she, shouldn't she? She looked tired, her shoulders were slumped.

Finally she rose from the table and said, "All right then." Together they walked about the room in search of his luxurious flat.

They found it. Willing hands dragged another desk out and set the two desks at a slight distance from each other.

The Mark of the play went over to the window-sill on which there was a large bottle which had once contained ink but was now empty. He poured wine into two phantom glasses and brought them over.

"Where is this man then," said Tracy.

"He won't be long," said Mark.

Tracy accepted the drink and Annie drank as well.

After a while Annie tried to put her hand around Tracy's waist. Mark the teacher glanced at the class: he thought that at this turn of events they would be convulsed with raucous laughter. But in fact they were staring enraptured at the two, enthralled by their performance. It occurred to him that he would never be as unselfconscious as Annie and Tracy in a million years. Such a shorn abject thing, such dialogue borrowed from television, and yet it was early drama that what he was seeing reminded him of. He had a quick vision of a flag gracing the roof of the "theatre", as if the school now belonged to the early age of Elizabethanism. His poor wooden O was in fact echoing with real emotions and real situations, borrowed from the pages of subterraneous pop magazines.

Tracy stood up. "I am not that kind of girl," she said.

"What kind of girl?"

"That kind of girl."

But Annie was insistent. "You'll not get anything if you don't play along with me," she said, and Mark could have sworn that there was an American tone to her voice.

"Well, I'm not playing along with you," said Tracy. She swayed a little on her feet, almost falling against the blackboard. "I'm bloody well not playing along with you," she said. "And that's final." With a shock of recognition Mark heard her father's voice behind her own as one might see behind a similar painting the first original strokes.

And then she collapsed on the floor and Annie was bending over her.

"I didn't mean it," she was saying. "I really didn't mean it. I'm sorry."

But Tracy lay there motionless and pale. She was like the Lady of Shalott in her boat. The girls in the class were staring at her. Look what they have done to me, Tracy was implying. Will they not be sorry now? There was a profound silence in the room and Mark was aware of the power of drama, even here in this bare classroom with the green peeling walls, the window-pole in the corner like a disused spear. There was nothing here but the hopeless emotion of the young.

Annie raised Tracy to her feet and sat her down in a chair.

"It's true," he said, "it's true that I know this man." He went over to the wall and pretended to dial on a phantom 'phone. And at that moment Tracy turned to the class and winked at them. It was a bold outrageous thing to do, thought Mark, it was as if she was saying, That faint was of course a trick, a feint, that is the sort of thing people like us have to do in order to survive: he thought he was tricking me but all the time I was tricking him. I am alive, fighting, I know exactly what I am doing. All of us are in conspiracy against this Mark. So much, thought Mark, was conveyed by that wink, so much that was essentially dramatic. It was pure instinct of genius.

The stage Mark turned away from the 'phone and said, "He says he wants to see you. He'll give you an audition. His usual girl's sick. She's got . . ." Annie paused and tried to say "laryngitis", but it came out as not quite right, and it was as if the word poked through the drama like a real error, and Mark thought of the Miracle plays in which ordinary people played Christ and Noah and Abraham with such unconscious style, as if there was no oddity in Abraham being a joiner or a miller.

"Look, I'll call you," said the stage Mark and the bell rang and the finale was postponed. In the noise and chatter in which desks and chairs were replaced Mark was again aware of the movement of life, and he was happy. Absurdly he began to see them as if for the first time, their faces real and interested, and recognized the paradox that only in the drama had he begun to know them, as if only behind such a protection, a screen, were they willing to reveal themselves. And he began to wonder whether he himself had broken through the persona of the teacher and begun to "act" in the real world. Their faces were more individual, sad or happy, private, extrovert, determined, yet vulnerable. It seemed to him that he had failed to see what Shakespeare was really about, he had taken the wrong road to find him.

"A babble of green fields," he thought with a smile. So that was what it meant, that Wooden O, that resonator of the transient, of the real, beyond all the marble of their books, the white In Memoriams which they could not read.

How extraordinarily curious it all was.

The final part of the play was to take place on the following day.

"Please sir," said Lorna to him, as he was about to leave.

"What is it?"

But she couldn't put into words what she wanted to say. And it took him a long time to decipher from her broken language what it was she wanted. She and the other actresses wanted an audience. Of course, why had he not thought of that before? How could he not have realized that an audience was essential? And he promised her that he would find one.

By the next day he had found an audience which was composed of a 3a class which Miss Stewart next door was taking. She grumbled a little about the Interpretation they were missing but eventually agreed. Additional seats were taken into Mark's room from her room and Miss Stewart sat at the back, her spectacles glittering.

Tracy pretended to knock on a door which was in fact the

blackboard and then a voice invited her in. The manager of the night club pointed to a chair which stood on the "stage".

"What do you want?"

"I want to sing, sir."

"I see. Many girls want to sing. I get girls in here every day. They all want to sing."

Mark heard titters of laughter from some of the boys in 3a and fixed a ferocious glare on them. They settled down again.

"But I know I can sing, sir," said Tracy. "I know I can."

"They all say that too." His voice suddenly rose, "They all bloody well say that."

Mark saw Miss Stewart sitting straight up in her seat and then glancing at him disapprovingly. Shades of Pygmalion, he thought to himself, smiling. You would expect it from Shaw, inside inverted commas.

"Give it to them, sock it to them," he pleaded silently. The virginal Miss Stewart looked sternly on.

"Only five minutes then," said the night club manager, glancing at his watch. Actually there was no watch on his hand at all. "What song do you want to sing?"

Mark saw Lorna pushing a desk out to the floor and sitting in it. This was to be the piano, then. The absence of props bothered him and he wondered whether imagination had first begun among the poor, since they had such few material possessions. Lorna waited, her hands poised above the desk. He heard more sniggerings from the boys and this time he looked so angry that he saw one of them turning a dirty white.

The hands hovered above the desk. Then Tracy began to sing. She chose the song 'Heartache'.

> My heart, dear, is aching;
> I'm feeling so blue.
> Don't give me more heartaches,
> I'm pleading with you.

It seemed to him that at that moment, as she stood there pale and thin, she was putting all her experience and desires into her song. It was a moment he thought such as it is given to few to experience. She was in fact auditioning before a phantom audience, she and the heroine of the play were the same, she was searching for recognition on the streets of London, in a school. She stood up in her vulnerability, in her purity, on a bare stage where there was no furniture of any value, of any price: on just such a stage had actors and actresses acted many years before, before the full flood of Shakespearean drama. Behind her on the blackboard were written notes about the Tragic Hero, a concept which he had been discussing with the Sixth Year.

"The hero has a weakness and the plot of the play attacks this specific weakness."

"We feel a sense of waste."

"And yet triumph."

Tracy's voice, youthful and yearning and vulnerable, soared to the cracked ceiling. It was as if her frustrations were released in the song.

> Don't give me more heartaches,
> I'm pleading with you.

The voice soared on and then after a long silence the bell rang.

The boys from 3a began to chatter and he thought, "You don't even try. You wouldn't have the nerve to sing like that, to be so naked." But another voice said to him, "You're wrong. They're the same. It is we who have made them different." But were they in fact the same, those who had been reduced to the nakedness, and those others who were the protected ones. He stood there trembling as if visited by a revelation which was only broken when Miss Stewart said,

"Not quite Old Vic standard." And then she was gone with her own superior brood. You stupid bitch, he muttered under his breath, you Observer-Magazine-reading bitch who never liked anything in your life till some critic made it respectable, who wouldn't recognize a good line of poetry or prose till sanctified by the voice of London, who would never have arrived at Shakespeare on your own till you were given the crutches.

And he knew as he watched her walking, so seemingly self-sufficient, in her black gown across the hall that she was as he had been and would be no longer. He had taken a journey with his class, a pilgrimage across the wooden boards, the poor abject furnitureless room which was like their vision of life, and from that journey he and they had learned in spite of everything. In spite of everything, he shouted in his mind, we have put a flag out there and it is there even during the plague, even if Miss Stewart visits it. It is there in spite of Miss Stewart, in spite of her shelter and her glasses, in spite of her very vulnerable armour, in spite of her, in spite of everything.

IN THE SCHOOL

THEY CAME IN to the school through a window, Terry handing the can of petrol to the other two who were waiting on the floor of the boiler-room down below. It was the evening of a fine summer's day, and the school was empty, for it was the holidays.

Terry, the mad one, walked along the corridor first, the other two behind him as they always did, and always had done. Usually Terry was shouting and playing about but tonight he was quiet, at least at first. It had been his plan, for he hated the school, he hated it with a bitter hatred and he wanted to destroy it. He hated the teachers, he hated his parents, he hated the whole world. He was a burning simmering fire of hatred, always on the edge of explosion, and it seemed to him that fire was the only answer to the fire inside him. Time and time again he had been belted, for he was either fighting other boys in the school— when the force inside him demanded violence, as if it were a demon from hell—or he was demanding money with menaces, for he was poor, or he was creating some novel or ancient kind of trouble in the classroom. The very last day of term he had fought a boy in the cloakroom and had broken his nose. The boy had looked at him that second too long, but it was enough. Terry hated anyone staring at him, as if he were a freak or something. He had been given six of the belt and that had been his farewell to the school, the headmaster standing at the door shaking his dim wormy head, the belt in his hand.

Terry hated the school because he didn't want to be there in the first place, especially after getting up in the morning to the interminable quarrels between his father and mother ("Get off my back," his mother would shout, "why don't you shove off?"), the crowded house where the other three children would fight each other as well. He never had any money or if he had it was money he had screwed out of pupils, usually first year ones, who did not dare to report him to their parents, and usually said that they had lost it. He had a job in Woolworth's for three weeks before he was found carrying a hundred cigarettes home, concealed beneath his jersey. Sometimes he would go into insane rages and beat his fists against a stone wall till the blood came.

He walked on, swinging his can, and suddenly out of the quietness began to shout obscenities, completely forgetting where he was or what the dangers might be: or maybe it was, thought Roddy, that he didn't care, that he wanted teachers to appear so that he could fight them.

The other two, Roddy and Frankie, followed him as they had always done, Frankie indeed imitating Terry's walk. Frankie was like a small cinder, ginger-haired and pale, without Terry's flamboyant madness but with hard deep cold eyes. The two of them admired Terry because he didn't care for anyone, and if he was belted he never cried, he held his hand out disdainfully as if belting were an awful bore which he despised. Nothing mattered to Terry, he was a spark of hatred, he was the king. Time and time again they had seen him do things that they themselves would never have dared to do. They had seen him square up to Baney, the Chemistry teacher, and Baney had backed down, only saying weakly that he would send Terry to the headmaster, but he never did. They had seen him break calmly in half the ruler the Mathematics teacher had given him and sit back in his seat arms folded. They had seen him setting fire to a girl's hair at the back of the Assembly when the headmaster had been going on about Jesus and the disciples who had been ordinary men. They knew very well what the headmaster had been really saying, they were the ordinary fishermen and the headmaster was one of the top ones like Jesus. They weren't stupid, they knew what was going on all right, they could read between the lines though they couldn't read the lines themselves very well. And that guff at the prize-giving by that fat git that there were some people who didn't win prizes but that didn't make them any worse than the ones who did: they knew just the same what would happen if their mothers or fathers tried to get on to the platform where the women with the flowered hats sat, and the men with the bald heads and blue suits.

They walked along the corridor as far as the Maths room into which they looked at the crummy equations which were still on the blackboard. The Maths room was not their target but nevertheless Terry urinated all over the boxes full of exercise books in the corner. He did this patiently and steadily, playing arcs of water up as high as the desk and then onwards as far as the door.

"Hey," he shouted to Frankie, "you get along to the Art room and get paper. We need paper for the fire. Piles of the stuff."

Frankie turned and went, for he was used to acting as Terry's message boy, he was like a legate sent to the provinces by his commander. The last they saw of him was when he swaggered through the door of the Maths room on his way upstairs.

After he had urinated Terry got a piece of chalk and first rubbing the equations off the board began to draw what purported to be the teacher's sexual organs in considerable detail. He spent the whole fifteen minutes on this, his tongue stuck out, absolutely concentrated on his task, as if he were an artist who had forgotten where he was. At times not happy with what he had done, he rubbed it all out, and began again. After a while he drew back from his masterpiece, studying it with an appraising scrutiny as if he were in an art gallery and said, "Hey, that's great, Rod, ain't it. Ain't that great?" Roddy nodded for unlike Terry he believed that too much talking was sissy and he modelled himself on Clint Eastwood. "Ain't that great," Terry said again and began to dance up and down among the boxes of books like a Zulu. Sometimes Roddy thought Terry was crazy, like the time he had jumped off the bus which was going at thirty miles an hour so that he wouldn't have to pay his fare, and he had rolled over and over on the street like a cat. In his phantom Mexican hat and lethal black uniform, Roddy wondered whether Terry would have done the same thing if a car had been coming, and concluded that he probably would have.

They left the Maths room, Terry giving a final look at his masterpiece as if reluctant to leave it, since no one would see it till the school started again after the holidays. The school was ominously quiet and it bothered Roddy though it didn't seem to bother Terry at all. Like Terry, Roddy was used to noise and movement, either the movement of the world outside—traffic, shouting, fighting—or the noise of the family in the crowded tenement where he lived. He hated total silence about him though he himself never talked much. He hated those periods of silent reading when that bag Simmons made them read *Kidnapped* or *Treasure Island* and you felt as if you could scream, the room was so quiet. The tension built up inside you so that you had to clench your teeth to prevent yourself from howling like a wolf. He wanted to stand up and throw a brick at Simmons, to kick her in, to flatten her long quivering nose. Sometimes she would look up from her own reading—for she read with them, 'to set a good example'—and a stare of naked hatred—the more bitter for being unseen by anyone except themselves—would pass between them across the room. Oh, he knew she hated him all right and she knew that he hated her. She didn't want people like him, she wanted people who were interested in books, who did what they were told, who sucked up to her in their new uniforms. Who cared about books anyway, the letters of the words were so hard to focus on. It was like trying to see the number of a bus on a wet day when the streets were glistening and your shoes and socks were soaking. The letters danced about in front of his eyes, like that red cloak he had seen them passing in front of the bulls on the telly, he would like to batter them stupid so that they would stay still. He identified himself with the bull, not the toreador, he would have liked to sink his horns into that dancing poof.

They stopped, this time outside the Gym, and as they did so Terry suddenly said, "Frankie's taking a long time. What the hell's happened to him?" And Roddy felt again that strange ominous silence of the school He suddenly had the weird thought, why don't they protect it, defend it? It must be because of something that he didn't know about. The entry had been too easy, the silence too prolonged. The school looked so defenceless, there had been no obvious attempt to keep people like him and Terry out. It was odd. They listened but they could hear nothing, not Frankie, not anybody. The stillness was appalling and the school was so clean, the floors were newly washed and there was a smell of disinfectant everywhere. The two of them stood there in the middle of the silence.

Suddenly Terry followed by Roddy turned into the Gym and that too was silent. From the stage end they looked down the length of the polished floor, at the tiers of slats which climbed the wall like a weir, at the ropes which were tied together, at the horse and the buck, at the box with the yellow footballs, at the roof with its acreage of glass.

Terry put down the can of petrol and said, "Let's have a game. One against one." And with his usual vividness and mad spontaneity he stripped off his jacket and shirt to make two goalposts at one end of the gym while Roddy had to do the same. Then they got a yellow ball out of the box and they began to play in the vast gym all by themselves on that summer evening. Terry did things like that—he sometimes forgot what he had come to do—but you couldn't cross him, he might turn on you and beat you up, out of the blue, or even knife you. You didn't know what he might do next, he was like a spark carried on a strange wind of his own.

Terry played like a madman with ferocious energy. He believed that he was a great footballer, though he wasn't, for he was too unco-ordinated. He believed that he was playing in the World Cup and that thousands of voices, like one, were applauding in an untranslatable language of their own. He pushed Roddy away with all his strength, committing every foul that was possible, at one time tripping him up as he was about to score.

"That was a penalty," said Roddy.

"Penalty my arse," said Terry, "you don't have penalties in a one to one, you stupid bugger." And the two of them stared into each other's eyes, but it was Roddy's eyes that fell first, confronted by the savage undeviating glare that shone out of Terry's gaze. At moments like these Terry seemed to forget who you were, that you were his mate, and he would be ready to do you. His whole body and his whole mind were concentrated on winning. He hacked at Roddy's feet when he had the ball, he elbowed him fiercely, at one stage he nearly bit him, and all the time he would be weaving up and down as he had seen players do in the World Cup.

Then after he was winning two-one he flopped down on the floor of the gym, and said, "That's enough. I'm shagged out." And he stayed there for a while, staring up at the glass roof where there was a small bird flying about, after coming in through a broken pane. It beat at the glass but it couldn't get out.

"Stupid bastard," said Terry, looking up at it. Roddy lay down beside him and thought that once he had lain like that in the past when his family had gone for a day to Loch Lomondside: and he had a memory of water flowing, and a few white clouds floating about like ice cream. Suddenly as they lay on the wooden floor Terry began to punch him and then the two of them were rolling over and over, kicking and gouging, till finally Terry was on top, his mad eyes glaring into Roddy's and it seemed for a moment as if he would choke him to death. Then the craziness drained out of his eyes and he got to his feet, put on his shirt and jacket and prepared to leave the room.

Roddy did the same. On their way out Terry retrieved the petrol can.

And then Roddy said, "Where's Frankie got to? Where the hell . . ." The silence enfolded them again, the eerie silence.

"Maybe the wee bugger's gone home," said Terry. "Maybe he didn't have the guts for it."

But Roddy wasn't sure about that. For a strange moment he thought he saw out of the corner of his eye a flash of black like a bird's wing passing, but that was impossible. That must surely be impossible.

"You go and have a dekko," said Terry. "You go. See if Frankie's there." No no no something deep in Roddy said. No no no and it was like the voice of a bird, a big black bird.

"Come on, Terry,' he said, "let's get it finished with. Get the petrol on and let's get out of here. Frankie's gone home, that's what it is."

But Terry was adamant. "No, you go and have a dekko." And he stood there solidly, the can still in his hand. "I'll be in Grotty's room. That's where we start it. Bring the paper. Bring Frankie and the paper. I'll be there. Right?" He was like a commander giving orders to his staff or to the troops. "You get along there."

And all the time the voice was telling Roddy not to go. The place was too quiet. There was something funny about it. There was no noise anywhere, not even a tiny creak. Even the slats in the gym, climbing up to the roof, had looked oddly still, and the ropes hanging down like snakes. And the buck standing in the centre on its own. Everything looked unprotected and waiting. There had been no real smell there as there used to be from the boys as they waited to start their exercises. There had been no human stink of dirty socks. There was only the neutral smell of disinfectant everywhere.

He stood at one end of the corridor glancing back at Terry and at that moment Terry looked like an ape swinging the can of petrol in his hand. Christ, what were they doing there, as if they had all the time in the world, as if they were on a visit or a tour of the place? Why hadn't they just put it on fire as they had meant to do? But this place was like a church, as silent as a church, but instead of incense there was only the smell of polish and disinfectant.

He was frightened. He should just turn and run but he couldn't because Terry was there and Terry would get him later, there was no escape from him. You couldn't get away from Terry. You hated and admired him at the same time. He himself hated Terry but in a different way from that in which the teachers hated him. He hated him because he had never beaten him. Even in the gym Terry had cheated and he had to take it because there was nothing else he could do. Terry made his own rules: for instance he had decided to stop playing when he was leading two-one.

Oh, bugger it, he must go and get the paper and if Frankie had been playing about, then he would do him. If he couldn't do Terry then he would do Frankie. He turned abruptly away.

Terry was laughing like a maniac at the far end of the corridor with the can in his hand.

Terry watched Roddy go. He would wait there till the two of them came back, he couldn't do anything without the paper. He stood against the wall and laid the petrol can down in front of him. He stared along the corridor and could see nothing, just the wall painted a bilious green. It was like the wall of a prison he had once seen in a film, blotched and patchy. He waited. He wished he had a watch but he didn't have one—he'd lost the one he had nicked from the jeweller's—other people had watches but he had none. Other people had football strips but he had none. Other people had hi-fis but he had none. He waited. And up above there was silence. He fancied for a moment that there were guards up there as there were in prisons on the films. No Frankie, No Roddy. For a second he thought he saw something flicker but no that couldn't be right. He waited and they didn't come. He knew that they could have gone along the top and down another stair and out of the school that way: perhaps the two of them had got the shakes and run home.

The buggers. Everyone left you in the end, even your mother and father. Everyone looked out for himself. If it hadn't been for his fire of hatred and strength he would have been ground down to the earth long ago. If it hadn't been for the rage that smouldered inside him and never went out, ready at any moment to burst into flame, he would have been finished.

You had to fight for yourself or people would get you. Or if they didn't get you they would betray you. You couldn't trust anyone. You had to fight for everything, for every scrap of property. Like that headmaster: he thought he was up there with Jesus and you were down here with the fishermen. They all thought you were stupid but it didn't seem to occur to them that you thought they were stupid. He himself wasn't stupid, he knew he wasn't stupid, not deep down inside himself. It was the stuff you had to do that didn't make sense. It made you scream with rage keeping you here doing things like Maths and English which didn't have anything to do with anything. He'd never

heard anyone speak like they spoke in the books. His father and
mother never spoke like that. And what were these triangles in
aid of. He'd never seen one outside school in his whole life.
Anyway he could sort his father out now. One night he had held
a knife at his throat when he was lying in bed. He had asked him
for money and his father had whispered, "You'll find it in my
jacket." He wouldn't have been able to do that if his father
didn't have a bad back.

He passed his hands over his eyes. He couldn't allow himself
to do that when the other two were there. They would think you
were weak if you told them you got headaches now and then.
You always had to show that you weren't weak, you had to keep
it up all the time. Bugger them. They must have gone home.
He'd just have to go to Grotty's room himself and hope that
there was paper there. Because they had betrayed him he felt
bitter: he felt as if he wanted to burn them down as well as the
school. He wanted to see them running like rats among the
flames like in that warehouse they had broken into one Sunday
and set on fire. There was nothing like a fire, it was so really
powerful, nothing could stand against it, it was great when you
made it yourself and you saw it coming into action like a servant,
especially in those old buildings when the rats ran about in the
flame and the smoke, and the little buggers didn't know where
they were going.

He walked along the corridor carrying the can in his hand
and arrived at the Latin room. He never took Latin, they said he
was too stupid, but one day when he was making a noise in the
room next to it, jumping up and down on one of the desks, the
Latin teacher, Grotty, had come in and taken him out and given
him six. He hadn't forgotten that, especially as the Latin teacher
didn't have people like him in his class, and he only took the
best, though he had belted him just the same after he had made
sarcastic remarks about him first in front of the class, using long
words that he didn't understand. Barbaric it was, he wouldn't
forget that.

He arrived at Grotty's room and looked round it. The desks
here were clean with no names carved on them, there were

pictures of temples and people with skirts on the walls, and on the board were words which he didn't understand. He went up and looked at them.

INSULA he spelt out aloud and then he spat at the word. What the hell sort of word was that? Who wanted to know about these bloody words, the other ones were bad enough. He spat again and again and then finding a black gown hanging on a nail pussy-footed about in it for a while like a poof or a ballet dancer, before finally tearing it into ribbons, sometimes using his teeth. He found a piece of chalk and scrawled stuff all over the desks and sometimes there were not only single words but sentences, almost the beginning of a story, his story. The only Roman he had ever heard of was Julius Caesar and he wrote on one desk JULIUS CAESAR WAS A POOF and burst out laughing crazily. It never occurred to him that no one would see what he had written.

Then in a frenzy of activity he began to gather desks together. He pulled at the handle of the weakest-looking cupboard till he opened it and a pile of old dusty papers—examination papers—came pouring out. He picked them from the floor and then put them inside the desks and prepared to pour petrol over them, but then a thought struck him and he got the wastepaper basket which was made of wicker, and put that in the desk as well, among the papers, standing out of them.

As he was doing this he thought he saw a black flicker again but paid no attention as he was too busy with what he was doing. The familiar lust was growing in him like sex. Sometimes the fire as it swirled and grew and changed shape was like a bint's body moving and curvaceous. It was like one of those bints you saw on the TV sometimes, advertising chocolate or a drink. He bent over the desk as if over an experiment and his mind was totally focussed on what he was doing. He was like a Frankenstein, he suddenly thought, and he flashed two of his teeth like fangs at the desk piled with papers. For the moment he had forgotten about Roddy and Frankie, he would sort them out later anyway. He would put the boot in. He was like a mad scientist bowed over the desk. He raised the can. And at that moment a movement flickered at the corner of his eye and he looked up. He turned and stared at the door and he saw him standing at the door in his black gown.

The man in the black gown was looking at him and the man in the black gown had no face, and the gown was dusty and had holes in it. Terry screamed and threw the petrol can straight at him as he ran for the door. He went through the dusty gown, right through it, and the can rolled along the corridor spilling the petrol as it went. It rolled along the polished floor. Terry ran along the corridor at full speed as if he were making for an invisible tape, his tongue hanging out, his eyes rolling in his head. Then at the end of the corridor he saw another man and he had no face either. Terry turned back and the other man, the one from the Latin Room, was walking towards him. Terry stood in the middle of the corridor not knowing where to go. Then he saw more and more of them. They were coming out of the classrooms, out of the walls, like huge black insects. All of them were in dusty black gowns and they had no faces or if they had they were the colour of chalk. Terry stood there and watched them, his breath going in and out. Steadily and unhurriedly at a grave pace they came towards him. He cowered down on his knees in the corridor. They made a ring round him and they looked down at him. He stared at his own hands which were beating like a fish against the floor. They stared down at him and they had no faces. He looked up and he screamed and he screamed and he screamed.

And his hands beat against the floor with all the life that was in them.

His hands beat on the floor in the silence.

MR TRILL IN HADES

ONE AFTERNOON Mr Trill, dead classics master of East-borough Grammar School, found himself in Hades.

The journey across the river had been a pleasant one, for the boatman had been fairly communicative though he had a small stubby black pipe in his mouth from which he exhaled meditative smoke rings across the water.

Mr Trill was quite happy to sit in the stern and now and again like a boy dip his hand in the quiet waves. Nevertheless he was quite excited and asked the boatman a few questions.

"Did you have many going over this morning?"

"No, not many to speak of," said the boatman.

Mr Trill was silent for a while wondering what sort of life this was, ferrying people from one side of a river to another, and perhaps not even having a holiday in one's whole life.

As if the boatman had understood what he was thinking he said helpfully.

"It's in the family, you see."

In the family? Did that mean that the job passed down from father to son, or did it mean that the whole family took alternate turns at the job? He imagined a great number of ferrymen, each wearing a cap like this and each smoking a black pipe, unless of course there were women who could also, he assumed, be able to carry out the task of being a ferryman.

"The class of passenger has gone down," said the ferryman. "You don't get the same type now."

"I can believe that," said Mr Trill and in fact he did believe it.

Even in his own school since comprehensive education the quality had deteriorated, and he hadn't been very fond of the last headmaster who was a large bearish barbaric man, a comedian among the dignified photographs of his renowned predecessors.

"I can tell the intelligent ones from the unintelligent ones," said the boatman pulling steadily at the oars. "You're one of the intelligent ones. You turned the board over so that I could see the white side, according to instructions. Some of the other ones wait there all day not knowing what to do. How am I supposed to know that they are there if they don't turn the board over? That is what I would like to know."

"That's very true," said Mr Trill. "That's very true," he muttered again.

"One of them," said the boatman, "stayed there all day and he hadn't the gumption to turn the board over though our instructions were staring him in the face. When I crossed over— because my son who has sharper eyes than I have saw him—do you know what he said?"

"No," said Mr Trill, "what did he say?"

"He said it was my job to make sure that he was there. You should be reported, he said to me. But I knew he didn't have any class. His suitcase had an old belt round it."

He was silent for a while and then added, "He was going to report me. You're all the same, he said, you ferrymen, lazy good for nothings. All you want is your obols and you don't care about the passengers. I suppose you'll be putting in for a rise next. I nearly told him to go to hell . . . but it didn't matter as he was going there anyway."

"I can see that," said Mr Trill who hadn't laughed, since he didn't have much sense of humour. When he was teaching he would stride into the classroom, the Vergil open in front of him, and without raising his eye from the book ask someone to read. Sometimes there might be a long silence and only then would Mr Trill know that the person whom he had asked to read was absent. He had a long Roman nose and a shock of gingery hair and the energy of a dynamo. His landlady thought he was crazy and he himself didn't like women or bingo. He had never married. His father had also been a classics master who had married a girl employed in the school canteen. She had taught him about carpets, curtains, furniture and paint.

"Well, here we are," said the boatman, "and there's your case."

Trill felt in his pocket but found he had no money for the trip.

"That's all right," said the boatman. "We're all on fixed rates now. Cheers."

He turned back to the opposite bank and Mr Trill stood on the one where he had landed and looked about him.

There was a lot of mist and he couldn't see clearly where he was but the air was mild and gentle.

He didn't feel at all hungry after his trip and it occurred to him that he wouldn't feel any hunger as long as he . . . as long as he was in the place where he was.

"Well, well," he said to himself, "this is very nice. Very nice indeed and I don't feel at all afraid as I did when I left for the first time to go to university." He walked forward and saw beneath him a valley in which he thought he could make out dim shapes here and there lolling about, some of them gazing into space.

He descended into it and found himself beside a number of people who were sitting talking to each other but who immediately stopped when they saw him.

One man with a red nose who seemed to be their leader asked.

"You new?"

"Yes," said Mr Trill, thinking of the boarding school of many years before, the dormitory, the cricket matches, the basins with cold water.

"Thought I hadn't seen you before. My name is Aphareus. Served in the Trojan War. . . . And my comrades here. The same."

"Course," he added, "we're on our own here. The officers don't mix with the privates . . ."

"What do you do with yourselves then?" said Trill.

"Do with ourselves? There's no need to do anything with ourselves. We're quite happy here aren't we, old pals?"

Seated on the grass the others looked at him calmly.

Mr Trill inhaled deeply and said, "You were in the Trojan War?"

"We were that, weren't we, old pals. We always stick together. Lived and died together. From Greece we all are."

Naturally.

Achilles, Agamemnon, Hector, Ajax, those marvellous heroes, they had seen them all.

"Course we saw them. Served under Agamemnon. Didn't know his arse from his elbow. And we got news what happened to him. Took ten years to get into that bloody town. Course we died before that, most of us."

What had it been like?

"To tell you the truth, they used to come out and we used to get out and fight them. There were as many gods there as soldiers, some taking one side, some the other. Most of the time we were pretty bored. Fighting, lying in bed, watching that wall for years, knew every stone of it. Course we had our own wall, too, all round the ships. All we wanted was to go home. But that was not to be. They had to make a wooden horse to get in there. I call that cheating but that was Ulysses for you. All he was interested in was himself. Bright as a needle, mind you, stocky little man. And there was old Agamemnon fighting with Achilles all the time, and bringing his own daughter out for sacrifice so that the ships could move. I'd have told the gods to stuff themselves 'fore I would do that."

"But . . ." said Mr Trill.

"Look around you, friend, whoever you are. Do you see that hill up there? That's where the officers are. They never mix with us, never talk to us. Have you had your entry noted yet?"

"No."

"They'll do that right enough. They know all about us. Amazing how they didn't put the tags on you. We think it's something to do with that castle but no one's ever been in it, no one we know anyway. Do you see it over there?"

When Mr Trill looked in the direction the man was pointing he saw a big shape swirling indecisively in the mist.

"There's a river there," said Aphareus. "People have tried to cross it. But they never make it. No one knows what's in there. They say they have hounds patrolling all the time. Anyway, who cares? We're quite happy here. But to get back to that lot, they were pretty punk, acting like women all the time. Like little girls. Imagine taking all that time to a siege. And all done by a trick in the end, not good honest fighting, spear against spear, but a trick. It makes me puke to think of it. No strategy, just stand there and slog it out all the time, or retreat to the ships, our side, or to the town, their side. Agamemnon didn't know how to handle Achilles, that was the trouble. If it had been me I would have sent him home with his tail between his legs, like a dog. Year after year we sat staring at that wall and year after year our children grew up and we never saw them. And the officers divided the women among themselves whenever they got any. And when did we privates get women or wine, I ask you. I remember when I got killed I didn't mind it, the time had felt so long. I didn't care when I saw the spear coming at me, it went right through my shield, of course I didn't have a shield with ten layers as Ajax had. And the Big Boss himself had ten strips of enamel on his with a snake on it. Isn't that right, fellows, I didn't care?"

They all nodded their heads as if they had heard the story over and over again and would never grow tired of it.

"I'll tell you something, we could have finished the war for them ourselves but who listens to the likes of us? Tell you about Agamemnon. He used to come round and speak to us now and again. You could tell he didn't have a clue, a big red-faced fellow, very hearty but false. Ulysses and Nestor, they were the ones who were really running the show. But Agamemnon, he was always smiling and waving from his chariot but he didn't have a clue. "You'll be home for the festivities," he'd say, "you trust me, lads." And we didn't trust him at all. And who stood there year after year though it had nothing to do with them? Us. What did it have to do with us, tell me that. A whore and a man who couldn't keep his wife. Paris, you know, was always firing arrows, you hardly ever saw him with a sword in his hand. I'm telling you I would have knocked Agamemnon off and gone home, only I didn't think of it at the time. But then Menelaus was his brother, it was all in the family, not that Agamemnon ever thought much of Menelaus, about as much as Hector thought of Paris. They told us it was a patriotic war, patriotic my arse, and then they told us that it would make us all richer with all the plunder we would get. But who got all the plunder? I'll tell you, it was the officers, and who got a spear in his guts if he fell asleep on watch? I'll tell you, we did. But how could it make us richer, I ask you. I had a little piece of ground and a wife and children. What did I want with Troy? Nothing. And when I saw that man with the spear I was so bored . . . I didn't mind. I wasn't at all frightened. And yet to die like that so far from home, with all these dogs feeding off you. . . . But the thing is that I didn't have any respect for Agamemnon. There he is up on that hill and Achilles sits on another hill. They hold court there and they never speak to each other except on a Friday. Hector and Achilles will speak to each other, funnily enough, but not the other two. And as for his daughter she's never approached him since he came here, though he was looking out for that. She's never forgiven him, he believed too much in the gods, you see. Rest of us didn't give a bugger. We're quite happy here, though, we don't mind. You tell him your story, Patroclus."

"Not the . . .?"

"No, no, this is a different Patroclus." And they all laughed as if they had made a good joke.

"It was like this," said Patroclus, a tall young fellow with glimmering fair hair. "One day I seen her standing at a little window which was in the wall. I don't know what I was doing there on my own."

"Picking daisies more than likely," said one of his friends and there was more laughter.

"Anyway I seen her and I knew her. I don't know how I knew but I did. She wasn't what I would call beautiful. She had a sort of thin face with high cheekbones and a cropped head. Not much flesh to her. But they say that she must have had it somewhere else, if you understand me. . . . Anyway she had Paris in a net. So I spoke to her. It was evening, late like. I just saw her there and everything was peaceful like, I went up to her same as I would go up to you and I said to her, Why don't you go back to Greece, just like that, I said to her. Why don't you go back to Greece? And all she said was, I wouldn't go back for all the world. And you could see she was enjoying herself. I wouldn't go back for all the world, that was what she said. Didn't I tell you that when I came back, lads?"

They all nodded their heads again, having heard the same story with avid hunger for century after century.

"I saw her plain as plain can be and she was standing looking out that little window and there was no blood in her cheeks at all, dead white she was, and I, thinking of all the lads here, said Why don't you go back to Greece? And all she said was, I wouldn't go back for the whole world. And she was smiling all the time and she spoke in that upper class accent. And then, do you know it came to me, I was telling the lads about it, I knew then that they was all enjoying the war, all these officers and captains, they was enjoying the war, the war was passing the time for them, and they was making names for themselves. . . . It was a short time after that that I was killed."

Amazed by what he had heard, Trill rose to his feet and left the soldiers. Was that then what the Trojan War had been like? Had Agamemnon known nothing of strategy? Had he just been a big red-faced fellow who was telling the soldiers that they would be home in time for the festivities? Surely not. Surely that was not what Trill had read in the big Latin and Greek translations when he was still young and his parents were as usual quarrelling.

"What is that boy doing sitting there day after day?" his mother would say. "And why is he letting all the other boys walk all over him?" Her beak snapped at him all the time while his father crept into his study for peace but even then she would put her snout round the corner and peck at him.

"And you too sitting in there reading and marking when there's painting to be done. When are you going to do something about the lawn and the garage?" And so he and his father would try to hide together in the study while the merciless fusillade stormed on. Carpets, curtains, ornaments, that was all his mother was interested in.

"All that rubbish that happened long ago, what is that to you?

You don't go out and meet people, that's what's wrong with you. You're living in the past."

And then she had started going to Bingo and he and his father had been left in peace, till she came home at night and then she would start again. "I met the headmaster's wife and she wouldn't speak to me. Who does she think she is? Just because I used to work in the school canteen she thinks she won't speak to me. I can tell her that I did a good day's work with the best of them instead of sitting on my bum as she does, drinking coffee all day. I had to work for my living and I'll have you know that. I didn't sit in my room all day reading about the past. Tell me, what are you going to do about the car? Are you going to trade it in or not? That's what I want to know and that's what you've got to tell me."

And her voice droned on and on and his father would look at Trill as if he was begging forgiveness for bringing his mother into the house in the first place. And Mr Trill would sit with his father as if he was his companion for he preferred to be with him than to be out playing with the rough boys who were always going on about sex and how long their things were.

That was at the beginning before he was sent to boarding school, but even then Mr Trill liked to haul out his big books from his father's shelves and try to read them.

"Why don't you get a proper big house," his mother would say to his father. "You've been in this house for years. I thought when we got married we would have a bigger house but no, not you. You just want to stay in this old house till they put you in a box and I'm ashamed in front of all the other teachers' wives. Why have they all got bigger houses than you? And why don't you put in for the headmaster's job? You've as much right to it as anyone else, isn't that true? You've worked hard enough. You slave there every night and no one can speak to you."

And the voice would continue, the beak would clack and the two, father and son, would huddle together in the study. And sometimes his father would tell him stories such as the one about Orpheus and Eurydice, and Mr Trill would listen with bated breath. What a tragic beautiful story, that lady moving about

Hades in white while Orpheus played his lyre to the cruel god.

And there he was. . . . For Mr Trill had wandered till he came to a sunny glade in which there were flowers growing and trees like the rowans that he had seen in the country when he and his father had gone for runs in the car. The berries were blood-red too and the tree leaned over Orpheus with all its pliant branches, and he was idly strumming his lyre.

No longer could Mr Trill see the soldiers, talking to each other, it was as if they had receded into the mist and left him alone in the sunlight with the singer. His heart nearly burst with joy as he thought of his father telling him that famous story when he was a child, allowing him to enter that golden kingdom for a while, evading his mother's sharp beak.

And here he was beside the singer in Hades, on a sunny hill with a river flowing past, black and complex as if it were a telephone talking endlessly to itself.

Orpheus, the sad singer, who had been so badly treated by Pluto, here he was in the . . . no, in the spirit, and Mr Trill could ask him questions, and talk to him. How astonishing that was, when he remembered the cutting voice of his mother who thought that history was finished with, and whose whole concern was whether a certain painting matched the paper on the wall, and who didn't believe in the existence of heroes like Orpheus. No, on the contrary, she thought that all history was a dream, that everybody had his weakness which she would find out in order to bring him down to the level of everybody else, including her own. She would pick holes in him, who did he think he was anyway? She wouldn't like to see anyone putting on airs and graces in her presence. For she was as good as Trill's father any day, and don't let either of them forget that fact or think they were any different just because she had worked in a canteen. She knew the world just the same and knew what people were like and she was more practical than his father in spite of all his degrees. Let them both put that in their pipes and smoke it. . . . And Mr Trill stood and watched Orpheus who was idly strumming on his lyre till the latter turned towards him a head which streamed with golden hair. How girlish the face looked, how white the skin. Mr Trill felt uncomfortable in the presence of the singer.

"I suppose you're another newcomer and you want to hear the story as well," said Orpheus petulantly. "Everyone wants to hear my story. It's part of the tour. Well, I suppose we might as well get it over with. . . . What do you know of it already? Some of them know a little and some a lot. And then there are all those old fat sweaty woman who go on and on saying, 'Poor boy, poor boy.' If only they knew how ugly I thought they were . . ."

Over his naked legs lay his lyre which he was strumming and Mr Trill said, "I know that your lyre was so entrancing that the stones and the beasts followed you. Isn't that right?"

"Yes, that's perfectly right," said Orpheus tossing his hair carelessly. "They did that. In those days I was certainly a good singer. . . . And then I married Eurydice."

"What do you mean?" said Mr Trill who was horrified to feel some doubt in his mind that this was really Orpheus for he didn't look at all like the singer as he had imagined him.

"Oh, it was nothing wrong with Eurydice," said Orpheus. "No man could have had a better wife. She was compassionate, kind, a good listener, a companion, and I loved her to excess." He paused and Trill said,

"Why then do you blame her? You seem to me to blame her."

"Blame her? No I don't blame her. There is nothing I can blame her for. If my friends visited me she was hospitable to them, and some of them were not all that reputable. Her love was flawless, perfect, there was no other woman like her. She was faithful, adoring, practical. If I wished to compose she would leave me alone, if I didn't she would talk to me. I never ever saw her angry. Would you believe that was possible; and yet I can tell you it was true. And at times I thought if she died that I would be helpless, without anchor, without rudder. If I came in drunk in the early hours of the morning she was always there waiting for me, but she never harangued me. . . . And then she was bitten by the snake and she died."

"And so," said Mr Trill, "you went to Hades to save her and bring her back to the world again."

"That is what I intended to do," said Orpheus. "I played to Pluto in that land of minerals, I charmed even Cerberus himself. I crossed with Charon in his boat and brought my lyre to the country of the dead. And Pluto said to me, "Now you can take her with you provided you do not look back." Such perfection she had had, such restfulness, such repose. And she looked at me with such trust and complete love. How can I describe it to you or to anyone else? She stretched out her arms towards me with such longing. At that moment even the darkness seemed clear and piercing."

"Well," said Mr Trill, "what happened? You were told not to look back and yet you did. Isn't that right?"

Orpheus seemed not to hear him but to be as it were listening to a voice deep within himself. "So much I thought of in that moment. Never before had I played so harmoniously, so finely, as when I was going in search of Eurydice, when I didn't have Eurydice at all. Do you understand that? It was as if my whole soul had become part Hades, part Elysium, it was as if I needed Hades. And for the first time ever I thought about my singing and my poetry, for never before had I thought of it. It had been as natural to me as the wind in the trees. I had not suffered any sorrow. It was as if at that moment I suffered an agony greater than any I had ever suffered, as if I had to cross over into the shadows, and become self-conscious. And that self-consciousness was necessary to me. Everything seemed to happen in that moment."

"What? What seemed to happen?" said Mr Trill. "I don't understand."

"I knew I didn't want Eurydice back."

"What?"

"That's true. I didn't wish her back. If you can understand this, her perfection was too great for me, it damaged my poetry. Do you know what I did then? I placed my art, the development of my art, before my love for Eurydice. I needed to suffer, it was in my nature to suffer. If I had brought Eurydice back, I myself would have died, I myself would have gone to Hades."

Mr Trill gazed at him uncomprehendingly.

"It was strange to see them with their bony hands pleading with me to save Eurydice: but what did they know of art?"

Orpheus crossed his naked legs disturbingly, and continued. "I had to suffer all that there was to suffer, know all there was to know. That was my destiny. And my destiny was unavoidable. From the very first moment that I had sung and played, I knew that my fate was to continue with my chosen art. And in Hades I felt that my power was greater than it had ever been, and that I needed a perpetual Hades. I needed an unending search for Eurydice. And all that happened in a single moment, as we stared at each other across the space of Hades, in that dimness of iron and ghosts. How can one ever describe that gaze? And let me tell you something else, the most bitter part of all, Eurydice knew what was happening, what had happened, and she agreed with me. She loved me so much that she agreed with me. She did not complain nor make any other sign of entreaty. Does that not in itself tell of her perfection? How could I ever have deserved her?"

And Mr Trill recognized that unalterable selfishness of the artist, that shield and armour which not even human feeling can pierce and he mourned Eurydice, and her implacable generosity. And he heard Orpheus' voice as if in a dream.

"And so I emerged into the upper world, and the stones were whiter than they had ever been and the trees were greener. And I wandered among the dead of this world, the perverted, the fallen. There is no den or hovel that I have not visited, there is no practice that I have not attempted. And all my songs have been elegies for Eurydice for she is the perfection that I have not attained. She had to die before I could possess her, and every song is a fresh attempt on her virginity, an interrogation of her love. Her love," he added hopelessly as if he did not know what the word meant.

"And I was determined that I wouldn't remarry. And so, well, I turned to others for my satisfaction, not women, if you get me. But they had their revenge on me in the end."

"What others?" Mr Trill was about to say when he saw Orpheus's melting eyes resting on him and it was for a moment as if he was lost in a mist of desire, languid and faint. Those white legs, those girlish hands and neck. . .

"I . . ." said Trill, "I . . ." It was as if he had entered a world which was dazzling yet corrupt, attractive yet unnatural, a total Hades of the spirit, in which Eurydice flowered poignantly among metals of a fierce flawed lustre. So this had been the reality of the story, this selfish passionate substance. For art to flourish, the human being must die, must stretch out its hands unavailingly, must accept death that another life be created, another music be made. Was there truth nowhere? Was every narrative ambiguous? Had the classic world been a deception?

"I . . ." said Trill again and got to his feet and ran away as fast as possible on his short stumpy legs, away from Orpheus who, as if he had already forgotten him, went back to his strumming again.

What a narrow escape, thought Trill, there had never been anything like that in Eastborough Grammar, though in the boarding school it had been different. But what was happening to his knowledge of the classics? It was as if everyone was determined to tell him the opposite of what he wished to hear and know about.

At that very moment Trill heard a voice saying, "Hullo, old chap," and he looked and there, standing in front of him, was Harris. Here among the shades, Harris whom he had hated so much.

"Well, well, well, so this is Rosy," said Harris, his flushed moustached face gazing down at him. "I often wondered what had happened to you. Little Rosy whose head I used to plunge in the basin."

"I'm going to run away," thought Trill feeling a trembling in his legs. I'm going to disgrace myself and run away. But he didn't. He stayed where he was, in the swirling mist.

"It's all right," said Harris. "I'm not going to touch you. As a matter of fact I'd be glad of someone to talk to. It gets boring down here and I never seem to meet anyone I know."

But Trill was seeing in front of him the faces of boys distorted with cruelty: he heard their laughter and felt again the cold harsh water on his face.

"Ah, those were good days," said Harris amiably. "Do you remember old Horace with his Latin and Greek. Silly old duffer. Never did me any good, that's for sure."

"What did you do then?" said Trill tremblingly.

"Oh, I went into business. No need for Latin or Greek there, I can tell you. Did quite well."

And his face faded and solidified, grew and withered.

"I don't believe you," said Trill in a high squeaking voice. "I don't believe you. You were always cruel and a liar. I don't believe that you did well at all. I believe that you were a—commercial traveller. That was all you were fit for. I hated you."

"Yes, I suppose you did. I suppose you did but we're both grown men now. We don't need to keep up that feud."

"We do, we do," shrilled Trill daringly. "Of course we do. Do you know that I had nightmares about you? Why did you torture me so much? I didn't do anything to you."

"Well, old boy, you looked so helpless, that was all, and it passed the time. God, those essays we did, and those rules. Lights out at ten. It was just that you were one of nature's losers, old boy, that's all. All you were interested in was handing in your comps all present and correct."

"But I didn't do anything to you and you used to put my head in the basin and tie up my bedclothes. Why did you do that?"

"I just told you. And anyway it's a long time ago. Why should you keep those grudges going? I bet you ended up as a teacher yourself. I can imagine you in the staff-room with your pipe in your mouth marking your exercise books and having a quiet look in class up the girls' legs. You were a bit of a sissy really. No offence. We always thought that."

"Who did? Who always thought that?" said Mr Trill, his voice rising to a scream. "Tell me that."

"Oh, if you want to know there was Ormond and Pacey and Mason, they all thought that. As a matter of fact, I saw Mason not so long ago. He's a brigadier now. But I haven't seen any of the others. I must say it's very lonely."

"Mason always said you were an old liar," shouted Trill, the blood mounting to his face. "He caught you out time and time again. He said that you would become a commercial traveller. You mark my words, he used to say, that stinker Harris will end up as a commercial traveller. And that was when Mason was in the Cadets. You were always trying to get out of them, weren't you?"

"They were so boring, old chap, so boring, all that dreary marching. So Mason said that, did he? What else did he say?"

"He said he thought your parents lived in the slums. He often told us that because he said why otherwise did your parents never visit the school?"

"Did he now?"

"Yes, and there were other things too. We once saw your underpants and they were full of holes. Did you know that we called you Holy Harris? We never told you that 'cos you were a bully."

"Well, well," said Harris his face fading and solidifying. "Isn't that interesting? You certainly find out things in Hades that you didn't know before. It's worth the visit. But surely after all those years you'll have forgotten about all that. I'll tell you what I'll do. I'll introduce you to some of the bigwigs. I've got a ticket here which allows you to see them. I can give it to you if you like. Would you like that?"

"No I wouldn't," screamed Trill. "I wouldn't. I don't want your ticket. You can keep your rotten ticket. You're a great big bully and you won't change and that's a fact." And as he looked Harris's face changed and wavered and the tears started to pour out of his eyes and his hands began to tremble and his whole body which had looked so imposing became small and withered, and even the striped tie which he still wore began to disappear.

"Please, please," said Harris holding his hands out in entreaty.

"No," said the implacable Trill, "no, no, no. I don't want to have anything to do with you. You're a bully and a cheat and a liar. And I can see your pants. Holy Harris, Holy Harris," he chanted, and the bony knees of Harris disappeared and there was no one left in the wavering mist but Mr Trill himself who groped about as if looking for his own body while the fog swirled around him and in the distance he could vaguely make out the lowering castle with its towers and battlements.

He looked down at his body to see if his own knees were still there or if he was still wearing his navy blue uniform with the badge of the red lion at the breast and the word SEQUAMUR written on it, but no, he was wearing his adult clothes—his suit greyed a little by the ashes of his pipe—and he was himself again, just as if he were the old Mr Trill sitting in a chair in the staff-room filling in the Ximenes crossword or interlacing essays with red marks as if they were bars of blood across the page.

At that moment he saw a tall figure looming towards him out of the mist, and he started.

"Who are you?" he shouted. "Do I know you?" But the figure passed on with a silent dignified walk. Mr Trill ran after it. "Who are you?" he shouted again and though he didn't realize it he looked silly running about with his case as if he were a business man whose train had left without his knowing it and who was scurrying about in search of the stationmaster.

The figure stopped and looked at him. It was tall and imposing and as its lineaments solidified Mr Trill saw that it was a woman, majestic, implacable. He went down slowly on his knees and heard himself asking, "Are you a goddess then? You are not Athene, are you? Or even Juno?"

"No, I am none of these," said the figure. "My name is Dido, and who are you?"

"My name is Mr Trill and I used to be a classics master at Eastborough Grammar, Dido," and he was almost overwhelmed that he had spoken her name but he began to speak again quickly and nervously. "I used to read poetry about you. 'And I shall know it even from among the shades.' You said that didn't you?"

"I can't remember. I suppose I might have done. I said many things." And the lips twitched with a brief pain.

"But your story," said Mr Trill, "can I not hear your story? Look, we are alone. We will not be interrupted. I've been told so much that I feel is wrong, and perhaps you could tell me the truth about yourself and Aeneas. Is it true that he left you and sailed to Italy? Is it true about the cave where you met?"

"Yes, it is true, it is all true. But what use is it to talk of it now? In his own mind he had his duty to do, he had to sail away and found Rome. That, he said, was his destiny. Who can resist the will of the gods? I thought we might," and her voice faded away. "It was possible that my love might, but it didn't. He sailed away secretly in his boats. Perhaps that was the worst of all. He should have told me."

"Perhaps," said Mr Trill daringly, "he could not bring himself to meet you again in case he could not continue with his destiny."

"Perhaps. What does it matter now? He has sought me here, I have seen him hesitantly lingering as if he wished to speak to me, but I, what should I have to say to him?"

"But the founding of a new city, of a civilization," said Mr Trill, "is that not more important than a private love? Rome became a great empire: it spread its power all over the world."

"Is that true?" said Dido in an uninterested voice. "Perhaps that is important."

"And then," said Mr Trill, "it produced a great poet who wrote about you. I think his sympathies were with you."

"With me? A Roman?"

"Yes."

As if talking to herself Dido said, "He charmed me with his stories. All the time that he was telling me of the fall of Troy, Carthage was being built. There was the sound of hammers everywhere. It was like a new beginning. I thought it would be a new beginning for us. But even while he was talking to me, even in the deepest moments of our love I knew that he was thinking of Rome."

"The poet says," Mr Trill persisted, "that it was with a heavy heart Aeneas left Phoenicia, though he was filled with love and longing."

"And I," said Dido, "was on fire when I saw his sails fading into the distance. It was as if I was burning. As a queen what should I do but kill myself? I had my own dignity too. Everyone has his dignity."

"Yes," said Mr Trill. And he was filled with hatred for that obstinate, god-obeying man who had set off in search of his own fame, leaving behind him a pyre that blazed on an abandoned headland. Was the creation of a new land, the pursuit of fame, narrow obedience to the gods, indeed greater than the love such a woman as this could give?

"There were some other words that the poet wrote," said Mr Trill, quoting from memory. "He wrote that you said,

" 'If that wicked being must surely sail to land and come to harbour because such is the fixed and destined ending required by Jupiter's own ordinances, yet let him afterwards suffer affliction in war through the arms of a daring foe, let him be banished from his own territory and torn from the embraces of Iulus, imploring aid as he sees his innocent friends die and then after surrendering to a humiliating peace may he not live to enjoy his kingdom in happiness: and may he lie fallen before his time, unburied on a lonely strand.' "

"I said that?" said Dido laughing. "When did I say that? How could I speak like that? No, that was not how I felt. How should love speak like that? How should I wish such things for him? I thought you said that that poet spoke well of me? What I felt was not that. When I saw those ships sailing away and I heard around me the sounds of the hammers as Carthage was being built, it was not vengeance I felt, rather it was hopelessness, as if my world was coming to an end. Have you not loved? Do you not know what love is?"

"Yes," said Mr Trill, "I have loved."

"If that is so then you must know that it is not anger one feels at such a moment." She paused and then began again as if she were back in Carthage, "It was a clear day and his men were pulling at the oars. Men were working around me excavating a harbour and others raising a temple and a theatre. The sea was so calm: it was the calmness of the sea that tormented me. He was sailing into the future and I was remaining there. Yet it was not anger I felt, it was the indifference of the day that tormented me. The sea was so calm, the day was so clear and pure and the ship was sailing away from me forever. Forever. And then I turned to the pyre and stabbed myself with my dagger."

Men and women, thought Mr Trill, the ambition of men, their daily task, and the love of women. The one who hunts and the one who remains behind. It has always been like that. There has been the searcher for new horizons and the one who keeps the horizons stable. Dido's foreign black face blazed out of the dimness and he was struck for the first time by the knowledge that this was a clash between civilizations. How had he never thought of it before? The fixed seeker after knowledge, the sensuous one who in spite of protestations did not care for destiny, for the unsleeping arrow of fame.

"Was I not married to him," said Dido, "if not in name then in love?"

So many shades flickered around them, hungry, unappeased, and Mr Trill could imagine Aeneas hesitating, trying to summon up courage to speak to her, ready to explain with quick words. But deeper than any words was this woman's knowledge: she knew that when the choice came he had chosen the abstract not the concrete, and nothing he could say would make her believe otherwise.

This queen, this marvellous queen, who blazed out of this dimness!

"I will tell you really what I felt," said Dido at last. "When I struck myself with that dagger I felt, Even if he should come back now, I would be dead and he would perhaps be sorry. I killed myself like any ordinary girl whose lover has left her: and I had thought I was a queen."

And she interrogated Trill with her marvellous eyes which shone like torches. "Imagine it, I had thought a queen would die differently from the rest of the women of the world. But no, it was just the same. His kingdom was to me a trivial thing, and his gods unimportant. When I thought, Perhaps he will see my pyre and know it for what it is, it was then my heart broke. Do you understand that?''

"I think I do," said Mr Trill.

"And do you understand, too, that that is why I do not speak to him. Words to him were everything. It seemed to me that I had listened forever to his words, and then it seemed to me that I had burned forever in that silence into which he sailed. I have thought much of that, that silence. It is now my weapon, as once it was his, on that day."

There was a calmness and Mr Trill gazed into the heart of it and it was as if in the very heart of it he saw a wound opening wide, and enlarging itself slowly and inexorably. Yes, he thought, it must have been like that, that is exactly how it must have been. On the fine clear warm morning, apparently full of hope, that is how it must have been. Her loved one left her, and she was alone, while all around her the city was being steadily built by workmen who whistled and sang as they worked. In the city that was being built Dido killed herself. And Mr Trill was filled with hatred for Aeneas, as if he were his own most bitter enemy, so that he could almost have shouted out to the departing ships, Don't you know what you are doing? Can't you see the heartache you are causing? What are you trying to do to this woman? Is Rome a sufficient prize for a broken heart?

But even as he looked Dido had faded away and in her place was. . . . Grace.

For ten years they had been going together, ten years during which he had taken her now to a classical concert, now to a theatre.

"Is it your night for going out then?" his landlady would say, her avid eyes fixed on him.

"Yes, Mrs Begg," he would answer.

And so he would put on his coat, take his umbrella and set off down the stairs past the window which showed the tiny green on which washing was drying in the evening light.

And Grace would be waiting for him outside the door of the

theatre or the concert hall, for she always arrived first. She was not at all pretty, he didn't expect that good fortune—nor indeed did he desire it—but she was pleasant, even-tempered, and always neatly but not showily dressed.

He would always buy her a box of chocolates though he himself wouldn't eat any, and after the play or concert was over they would go to a restaurant for their coffee and discuss the entertainment they had just seen.

"I didn't like his interpretation of Prospero," or "I felt that Miranda was just right," Grace would say, for she taught English. And Mr Trill, whose knowledge of English literature was not great, would listen to her, puffing at his pipe and feeling amiable and contented.

He was not allowed to go to Grace's home, for her mother, who was still alive though old, had, according to her daughter, a nasty habit of insulting any men she brought to the house, especially one in the far past who had ridden a motor bike and worn a helmet which he laid down negligently on the sofa when he entered the room. Though a clerk he had a careless taste for adventure.

Mr Trill never kissed Grace, for he regarded his friendship with her as belonging to an equable maturity without emotional storms or tantrums. He was glad in a way that her mother existed for she would save him from having to confront the problem of marriage to her daughter. Now and again Grace would refer to a house as if it were quite settled in her mind that the two of them would one day live together, but Mr Trill would pretend not to hear such remarks. Their friendship, he believed, belonged to the world of the mind, and he was happy that it should remain there, and that her mother should like Cerberus guard her house so that he would be unable to enter it.

Thus, as they strolled along in the gentle evening light after the play or concert was over, Mr Trill existed in a mild radiance of the mind and spirit, feeling himself superior to all those men who for some reason which he could never understand were involved in passionate quarrels with their sweethearts or wives. Sometimes he would read in newspaper that a girl had stabbed her lover in a jealous rage and he couldn't understand how this should be. Why did secretaries sob all day in offices when their boy friends had spoken a casual cruel word to them? Why did some of them kill themselves, or send vicious rancorous letters which dripped with poison and anger? Mr Trill himself didn't live in that world nor did, he was sure, Grace.

And so all was tranquil and peaceful and Grace was always equable and mild till her mother died suddenly of a heart attack. At first Grace had been prostrated and Mr Trill had sent some flowers. He had asked if there was anything he could do but she had told him that there wasn't, that it was really the sort of situation that he wasn't equipped to deal with: and he had blessed her perspicacity and thoughtfulness. Thus he did not learn anything about the mechanics of dying: he remained ignorant of the irrational guilt which Grace felt at actions done and left undone, he did not see her wandering about the house picking up a handkerchief of her mother's and then dropping it as if it were electrified. He did not see her sitting in church weeping while the coffin was being borne on the shoulders of four men to the waiting hearse. All these things had passed without his knowing them, nor did he see her on the sofa at night, her jotters abandoned at her side, while she shook with sobs or stared dully into space, knowing that there are things in this world which cannot be corrected.

The weeks passed and then they went out for the first time after her mother's death, to a concert given by members of the Cairo Conservatoire. As they sat in the second row watching the Egyptian conductor enter, and with a stern military gaze around the orchestra, invite them to a typically stormy Beethoven piece, Mr Trill knew that matters would never be the same again. He sensed that Grace's easy-going amiable nature had vanished and that contained within her was a storm of her own. Thus as the violinists rested their bows, though the trumpets sounded, he felt a chill in his bones as one sometimes does at the beginning of autumn: for Grace was silent and had refused the chocolates he had offered her. After the concert she invited him to her house but he refused to go as he said it was rather late and he still had some translations of Ovid to mark.

"So," she said pulling on her gloves, as they stared at the empty cups in the restaurant, "what are we going to do?"

"To do?" Mr Trill echoed, though he knew perfectly well what she meant. For a moment he was reminded of the story of Echo and Narcissus, how Echo had fallen in love with Narcissus but he had scorned her and she had faded away bodilessly into the depths of the wood while Narcissus sickened and died for love of his own ailing reflection.

"So are we getting married or not?"

"Getting married?" Mr Trill repeated.

"Yes, getting married. Are we or are we not getting married?" Her voice which had once been mild and amiable had suddenly grown harsh like the voice of a seagull that screams along the shore.

"I . . ." began Mr Trill.

And then she had begun. It had not occurred to Mr Trill that this woman who had been in the past so tranquil should so suddenly become violent and stormy, bitter poisonous words pouring out of her mouth.

"Well, are we or aren't we? I have been going out with you now for ten years and you have never mentioned marriage once. It is true that you couldn't very well do so while my mother lived but now that she is dead I don't see why we shouldn't discuss it."

Mr Trill thought it was rather indelicate of her to speak of her recently dead mother at such a moment and especially in a public restaurant but all he did was take his pipe out of his mouth, empty its grey ash into the ashtray and put the pipe back again into his pocket.

"Naturally," she was saying, "I believed that after ten years we could get married. Why else would I have gone out with you for such a long time? There were others I could have gone with but I chose to stay with you because I understood or thought I understood that marriage was in your mind, though we didn't discuss it. But now I want to know one way or the other especially as I deliberately protected you from the ugliness of death because I knew that you are not interested in such matters." Her eyes which had been so mild were blazing with temper and it was almost as if he were seeing a woman transformed into a demon in front of his eyes. Such must once Medea have been like when tormented by her love for Jason, and a pleasurable feeling trembled within him.

"I . . ." he began but before he could say any more she had risen to her feet and said, "I know you now. You are afraid of marriage, of the world. All you want to do is sit in your corner with your books. As long as you have your stinking pipe and can discuss a concert or a play with me that is all you want. Naturally. I'm thirty-five years old and now I find," and here she burst into tears though the restaurant was full of people "now I find that you don't care." Mr Trill looked around him with trepidation. Why, she was just like his mother, making a scene in public. She had the same unreasonableness. Could she not have waited till they had left the restaurant at least? But she didn't wait and she continued through her tears,

"All that time I was deceiving myself. I thought that when my mother died. . . . But no. Not you. Not once have you made any single gesture or shown any tenderness. Anyone else would have demanded that he help with the funeral arrangements. But not you. You simply agreed with what I told you. Go back to your landlady then if you like her so much."

This last statement astonished Mr Trill who had never thought of his landlady as other than his landlady, and who ate so little that he was hardly in the dining-room for more than ten minutes at a time gulping his food while his landlady who, he thought, knew nothing about his personal life brooded darkly about him and hoarded up the crumbs of information that he ignorantly gave her. What was Grace implying and why had she changed so much? It was as if he were listening to his mother again as she shouted at his helpless father who was trying to hide in his study.

"Please, Grace," he said, "can we not . . . ?"

"No, we can not. And don't 'please' me. I have asked you a question and you have given me your answer and that's it." All the time she was saying these words her pleading eyes were

gazing at him as if belying the sentences that she was uttering
and he saw her as she would be, a woman whom marriage had
forever passed by. Nevertheless though he recognized this with
his mind he didn't feel anything, nor had he any desire to touch
her or comfort her. It was as if there was a cold glacial being at
his heart like a tiny snowman who was gazing at this woman,
and seeing her as having no connection at all with himself. And
it occurred to him how extraordinary it was that one should
have feelings, that one should laugh and cry, that one should be
shaken by rage or jealousy. He felt fumblingly for his pipe but
then left it where it was.

Then she left the restaurant, her white shawl round her
shoulders, and he remained sitting where he was. At that
moment he felt desolate as if something valuable were leaving
him forever but at the same time he still made no effort to pursue
her. After a very long time he got up and walked slowly home.
The streets were yellow with light, the scholarly lamp-posts with
their bent backs leaned over the pavement as if studying it, and
Mr Trill trudged to his lodgings. He was tormented by an
absence, for never again, he felt, would he be able to discuss
concerts and plays with anyone in an atmosphere of peace and
tranquillity. Never again would he have his evenings to look
forward to. His landlady would ask him if he was going out and
he would have to answer that he wasn't, and then her little eyes
would glitter and she would begin to dig down into his life with
her little wicked spade to find out why he no longer left the house
on a Friday night as he had used to do. He would be naked to the
world, without armour. But he gritted his teeth and walked on
not even pausing to consider whether he should 'phone Grace in
order to find out if she had arrived safely. He vaguely thought
that she might kill herself but dismissed the thought immediately.
That would not at all be like Grace. That night he lay in his bed
sleepless and it was as if the room began to close round him, as if
some grief, hitherto invisible, was drawing closer to him,
ensconcing itself among his Greek and Latin books and casting a
sad light over his jotters.

Grace never married, and continued with her teaching, her

temper becoming more bitter and enraged. She still lived alone, as far as Mr Trill knew, in the house from which her mother had departed and among those yellow lights that seethed about the streets.

For a long time Mr Trill wandered about, after his meeting with Dido, confused in his thoughts and wondering if all his work on earth had been wasted, for he remembered with pleasure not unmixed with pain—especially in his latter years—the time he had spent in teaching. Some pupils he recalled with affection, some with dislike, but in general he was highly pleased—or had been until now—with his sojourn on earth, and with the work he had done there. And it was while thinking these thoughts that he came through the mist on a rugged hill and saw a man rolling a huge stone up it, his cheeks bloated, his teeth gritted. Whenever the man pushed the stone up the slope with great effort it rolled down again to the bottom, as if it were an animated being with a will of its own.

Why does he not stop, why does he keep on doing it? thought Mr Trill, as he watched in silence the man who hadn't noticed him. And of course he knew perfectly well who it was, it was Sisyphus.

And he knew also why he was doing it, it was because he had been condemned by the gods to do it. Why else would a man spend all his days and nights pushing a big boulder up a hill when it always rolled back relentlessly again? The gods, thought Mr Trill, the gods are our destiny. It is they who decide what we must do, and who keep us at it.

And yet he didn't wish to accept this reasoning. Was it the gods who had decided what he must do with his own life, what in fact he had done with it? Was it the gods who had decided what his father and mother must be like? Was it the gods who had decided that he must be born of such a mother and such a father, and that because of them he must do what he had done? Was the whole world, then, a huge machine, a huge boulder, dumb and bare, to which no one could appeal?

And, after all, had that not been the case with Achilles? Had

he not been told that after killing Hector he was doomed, and
had he not done it in spite of that?

And was it the gods who had decided that on a certain day he
should arrive at Mrs Begg's house, lay his case down on the mat,
press the bell, and that he would, after her acceptance, stay in
her house for thirty years? Had all that been decided by the gods?
Ah, Mrs Begg, were you too an instrument of the gods, with your
pride in your house, your incessant scourings and washings,
your ear for scandal, your meanness with fire in winter, and even
with sugar during all seasons? Was there some god that decided
that you and I should meet and perhaps made you think after
my break with Grace that I should perhaps get married to you
even if you had a moustache? Was it a god that guided me to
Eastborough Grammar School on that day when my heart beat
so strongly and I entered those alien gates and I laid my briefcase down for the first time in the staff-room and I hung up my
coat for the first time on its predestined nail and I read the
notices on the notice-board.

Is that so, thought Mr Trill as he watched Sisyphus make
another effort with the stone. The mist gathered around him
and there was Sisyphus in the midst of it pushing and moaning
and grunting and then just when it appeared that the stone had
reached the top it fell down again: and Sisyphus would stare at it
for a long time and instead of giving up would summon all his
energy and push and heave and grunt again while the muscles of
his jaws stood out and his arms strained and his back bent into
an arc and the brute stone without consciousness would almost
grinningly confront him. How sick surely he must grow of that
stone, without perfume, without grace, how he must hate and
curse it. But, no, Mr Trill did not hear a word of anger, it was as
if anger had been drained away over the centuries, as if long ago
Sisyphus had forgotten the reason for anger, knowing that the
stone would not hear him, nor the gods forgive him. How
strange, thought Mr Trill, as he sat and watched him, how futile
and odd. And as he watched he thought of the vanity of his own
life. First of all there had been the quarrels with his parents—
perhaps fated to meet each other—then there had been his

sufferings in boarding school, then there had been his years of teaching, and in the middle of these his break with Grace.

Had it all been like the stone and Sisyphus then? Certainly, perhaps, the last years had been, though not the middle ones. In the last years it seemed that he had lost his love for his work, it seemed that the teachings of the classics had fallen heavy from his lips. But before that it had been different.

The horror of it all, this Sisyphus and the stone! And then Mr Trill did a strange thing. He leapt down from where he was and began to help Sisyphus to push the boulder. Side by side they pushed, side by side they puffed and panted, and almost they had reached the top. Next time, thought Mr Trill, surely next time will do it. Nor was he afraid that he would be attacked for what he was doing. All he thought of was that he could not bear to see this useless toil. We will do it next time, we really will, he told the silent Sisyphus: and then you can stop your work and you will be happy.

This time a really big push will do it.

Damn you, he shouted at the stone, while Sisyphus grunted and puffed, a gigantic yet curiously insubstantial figure in the mist. Damn you, damn you, we'll get you this time, bald senseless thing. Push push push till the veins stand up on your forehead. Work work work till all the examinations appear easy. *Amo amas amat. . . . mensa mensam mensae mensae mensa . . .* O table, O chair, O stone . . . let life enter you, let you wing your way about Hades, fly about squeaking like a bat. Run about in the park, sing, dance. . . . And he pushed as hard as he could and he shouted as he pushed and then, glory of glories, the two of them were up on the sunshine of the hill with the stone and it was lying there on the summit as if it was where it had always wanted to be. They stood there amazed, Sisyphus still in silence, his arms hanging at his side, the veins on them swollen and blue. Ah, ha, we got you at last, said Mr Trill, giving the stone a kick and only succeeding in hurting himself. You big, stupid, senseless dolt, you ignorant, inanimate lump. As Mr Trill triumphed over the stone and made as if to shake hands with the weary shade the latter looked at him with infinite sadness and then very slowly and carefully pushed the stone downhill again and Mr Trill heard it thundering and banging till at last it came to rest though echoing still with a loud thunderous sound. Then still without a word, Sisyphus descended the hill and prepared to begin his endless task again, while above him Mr Trill sat and thought.

On his green bench Mr Trill sat and thought. At first when he had retired from school he used to sit in his room reading but then as time passed he realized that Mrs Begg was growing more and more irritable when she saw him there (and sometimes he would have to leave it so that she would be able to bring her hoover and clean the floor).

It was strange how Mrs Begg's attitude to him had changed. In the beginning she perhaps thought that there was a possibility of marriage, and for this reason she would tell him fragments of the story of her life. (Her marriage to a train-driver who had died of a heart attack: she, still, according to herself, could get free railway passes to any part of the country that she wished to go to. However she never went anywhere, not even to her nieces and nephews in Surrey.) Mr Trill hardly ever listened to any of her stories or if he did it was only with half an ear and even now after thirty years with Mrs Begg he didn't know the names of any of her relations, or what they did, though he had been given the information often enough in the moments between soup and mince or while he was drinking his tea. Nor did he really know much about Mrs Begg herself. She existed for him in a vague world as a being which as far as he was concerned had no emotions of its own, no ambitions or destinations, merely a servant who was there to give him, in return for money, the little food that he required.

He never for a moment realized that even in Mrs Begg's heart there beat storms of rancour as when for instance he ate absentmindedly without comment or even left half finished on his plate a particularly fine pie that she had specially made for him: nor did he notice that some days she had tidied the room particularly well, or even left a vase of flowers in it. On the contrary she was like a slave belonging to Greece, a manual worker who allowed him, the lord, to conduct his silent speculations.

Thus it was when he left the school he found for the time a cold wind blowing around him as if Mrs Begg had decided that he would never leave and therefore she could treat him as she liked. She sometimes grunted when he spoke to her and made references to the sunniness of the weather, and would howl about his legs with her hoover when he was deep in Homer. Therefore Mr Trill took it into his head to leave the house in the mornings and only come back at dinner time: and as he was a creature of habit he always departed at half past nine.

The park was a large one with plots of flowers scattered here and there. In the middle of it there was a fountain in which a Cupid composed of white alabaster hovered, bow and arrow in hand, while waters poured endlessly out of its mouth. Here Mr Trill would sit on a green bench and watch the world go by. Sometimes an old man would come and sit beside him and the two of them would discuss questions of the day or rather the other man would talk and Mr Trill would half listen for he had no interest in politics and rarely read a newspaper.

"The country is going to the dogs," successive old men would tell him. "Even the young people aren't frightened of the police nowadays. They throw stones at you and shout names and what does anybody do about it? Nothing. It wasn't like that in the old days."

And so he would listen to the same story, repeated over and over in various guises and various accents, of a world that was always peaceful with calm blue skies and perfect behaviour. And he would grow tired of it all but he didn't want to cause a disturbance, so he would agree wordlessly, now and then nodding his head, but in truth weary of it all.

"I am becoming an old man," he would think. "And is this what I wanted from my life? Is this where I wanted to be?" And sometimes he wished that he had married Grace and at other times he was glad that he hadn't done so. But most of the time he simply felt lonely.

Once he had gone up to the school, and swore that he would

never do so again. It wasn't that anybody had been unkind to him—on the contrary everybody had been very gentle and considerate—but it was as if they were talking to an invalid, as if their voices echoed around him with hollow solicitude. While they were talking to him, he sensed that they thought of him as an intruder, a sort of ghost who was no longer involved in the heat and the smoke. And even while they were speaking he felt them, as it were, glancing at their watches as if they were thinking how much they had to do, and that this old buffer was preventing them from getting on with it. The staffroom was no longer his staffroom, he himself had been replaced by a new younger man with fresh ideas, and he felt that he was a posthumous being moving about the circumference of the field on which the war was being waged. Even his old room had changed, it was less tidy than it used to be, there were pictures on the walls, and the desks were carved with new names.

So he decided that he would stay in the park and watch the flowers and if necessary endure the stories of the old men who were so implacable, stubbly and envious.

One day a little girl came over to talk to him. She had been playing with a paper boat in a pond but after she had finished she stood in front of him gazing at him with wonder in her eyes as if waiting for him to speak to her. But he found that he couldn't think of anything to say. If she had been older he might have offered to help her with her Latin—for that was all he could do—but as she was only four or five years old such an offer was out of the question.

Eventually she sat beside him on the bench swinging her legs and offering him her boat which he had looked at with surprise, unable to think of anything to say about it except that it was pretty.

"What is your name?" she asked him directly.

"Mr Trill," he answered.

"My name is Margaret and my mummy is coming to get me. She is at the shops." There was a long companionable silence while Mr Trill searched for some words to say to her but there was nothing at all that he could think of: not a single idea came

into his head. In front of him the flowers blossomed and the
gardener gazed at them, rake in hand, while the white Cupid
with bow and arrow leaned gracefully into the blue day.

The little girl swung her legs which were clad in white socks.
And Mr Trill gave her some sweets.

The following day she came back and the following day again
and Mr Trill finding nothing to say gave her more sweets and
she seemed quite happy to sit there beside him. Sometimes she
brought a doll and sometimes a teddy bear and there the two of
them would sit, Mr Trill now old and greying, looking out at the
park, and the little girl clutching her doll with the red dress and
the startlingly blue eyes which stared unblinkingly out of the
polished glaze of the face. And all the time Mr Trill was silent.
The world of children was forever closed to him for he hadn't
really understood them though he had taught them. To him
they were beings who must be instructed in Latin, they didn't
have minds or will or souls of their own. Nevertheless for some
unfathomable reason the little girl came and sat beside him in
perfect peace though now and again she would abruptly leave
him in order to float her boat on the pond and talk to the
gardener who seemed to have more to say to her than Mr Trill
had. Sometimes she would take him into her confidence and tell
him little snatches of her worldly affairs, though they were so
difficult to understand that Mr Trill would let his attention
wander, and indeed once she had stood in front of him stamping
her feet and saying how stupid he was. Mr Trill had accepted
this verdict quite calmly and without rancour as if it had a
perfect justice of its own.

Once he had made a great effort—as if speaking were like the
lifting of a great stone—and asked her where she stayed but he
couldn't make out the answer and had left the question dangling
where it was in the bright light.

She had even asked him whether he had a mummy or daddy
but Mr Trill had pretended not to hear: it would have been too
difficult for him to explain to her that they were both dead.

One morning when as usual he had sat down on the bench
which happened to be rather damp as it had been raining the

night before, a big man with an angry red face strode towards him. Mr Trill knew at once that he didn't belong to the middle classes, but rather to the ranks of the labourers. For all he could tell he might have been a miner or a bus driver or a dustman but he certainly didn't belong among those who work with paper and pen and ink.

"You the fellow who's always giving my daughter sweets," said this craggy-faced apparition standing threateningly in front of Mr Trill and clenching and unclenching his fists as if he was prepared to hit Mr Trill on the nose there and then.

"I. . . ." began Mr Trill. But before he could say any more the man—whatever his occupation was—had said,

"Well, I want it stopped. Right? Stopped. You understand." And his stony head came quite close to Mr Trill's. "Stopped you understand. Right. Kaput." And Mr Trill had nodded his head violently whereupon the man had also nodded two or three times saying

"I know your sort, mate," and then had marched away leaving Mr Trill in a stunned silence. From that day on the little girl came no longer to the park and Mr Trill had to listen to more nostalgic commentaries on the age from old men—and sometimes old women with shopping baskets—and felt more and more lost and weary. It occurred to him that perhaps he ought to have been more combative when faced by the stony-headed man, perhaps he should have said that he wasn't going to be pushed around by the likes of him, but Mr Trill knew that he wasn't the sort who would ever say any such words and so he declined into melancholy and despair. He had never fought back when he was in school and he would never do so in his old age. But what terrified him most of all and prevented him for a while from returning to the park was that the stony-faced man had simply seen him as a dirty old fellow who was quite prepared to make a sexual assault on his daughter, even though he was wearing a good suit and perfectly good shoes and was a scholar who knew about Homer and Vergil.

The unfairness and injustice of life! Could the man not have seen that he wasn't like that at all but was on the contrary a person of refined tastes who knew Latin and Greek and would never have lifted a finger to touch his child? Was that not entirely visible to him as Mr Trill sat there on the bench. But evidently it hadn't been, evidently he had been assigned to a room in the man's mind in which old men, whoever they were and no matter what their occupation or past history, behaved like sexual maniacs whenever they saw a little girl.

How unfair, how unjust.

I am growing old, thought Mr Trill, I am growing old and tired. Autumn with its chill airs is gathering round me and its breezes are about to waft me to the place to which all men and women go in the end.

And so Mr Trill ceased to visit the park and was never quite the same again. When he went out it was to sit in the library among the other old men and stare with blank wonder at the busts of the big-nosed Romans that were perched on top of the shelves, while a newspaper lay neglected in front of him on the sloping table. And finally he never left the house at all.

As Mr Trill walked along it seemed to him that he did not feel at all tired. The air was mild, though not invigorating, and he felt as if he was strolling in the twilight through a fair, though here there were no bright lights. What had happened to that other girl whose name he could not now remember, whom he had once walked with in just such a balmy twilight when he was in university so long ago? Where had he met her? It must have been at one of the Greek or Latin classes. She was the first girl he had ever taken out. Or had he simply met her at the fair? She had, he thought he remembered, blond hair, and she had turned out to be a good shot with the crooked rifles that they supplied there. What had she won again? A plate was it, or a little doll? Something cheap anyway. They had gone on to the big wheel, he, Mr Trill, erect and dignified, turning over and over, spinning like a top, his heart in his mouth, while she had looked at him with a joyful triumphant smile. How difficult it was to grasp the past, and remember oneself as one had been. Continually one lifted photographs from dusty tables and the faces were like ghosts, inquiring, young, hopeful, belonging to an irretrievable world that one would never see again.

No, he could not remember her name, but she had been a student, that much was clear to him. He remembered her eye squinting along the rifle, the ducks marching placidly in line, and she picking them off one by one till they had dropped and fallen away. And all the time there had been that tremendous vulgar music, the rotation of clusters of coloured bulbs, the stands decorated with classical motifs, faces of wolves like those which had been involved in the foundation of Rome. The wheels turned dizzily in the twilight and the girls and boys passed by with vaguely white flowery faces, as if they were blossoms set on invisible stems. Had he been happy that night? Was that why he remembered it? He had rolled pennies across boards but they had never come to rest on the proper numbers: he had tried the darts but they had missed their targets. And all the time she had been at his side, laughing and happy. How long ago it all was. Had he ever really been at the fair or was it all part of his imagination? As the days darkened so the lights brightened, so the sharp-eyed women behind the stalls came into clearer focus as they handed out their fixed and corrupt guns. And even when she had won her prize how cheap it was. Yet the crooked rifles were raised to eternally hopeful eyes, the big wheel rose brilliantly over the horizon, the coins spun across the slanted board. The fattest woman in the world, the haunted house, the train-ride through the tunnel. How carelessly people spent their money as if it would last forever while the voices shrieked with happy laughter. In spite of the fact that one knew at every moment that one was being cheated, that the odds were stacked against one, that every gun was crooked, every dart was the wrong weight, that it was only by a colossal fluke that one won even the tawdry presents that stared so cheaply out at one —nevertheless one spent money like water, like a king, for a sordid little cardboard plate, or a picture of an unreal spring.

And then the slow walk home through the twilight as if one were swimming. He remembered standing with her—whoever she had been and whatever her name—under a blue light which illuminated the porch of her house. Her face turned blue in the light and beyond the porch was the garden with its flowers wet with dew. The big house towered above him, it was late, and there were no lights in the windows. It couldn't have been lodgings, it must have been her own house. Was his own face as blue as hers? In the distance he could hear the noise of a bus fading. Otherwise there was complete silence.

What had they spoken about?

"Thank you for a lovely evening."

"Thank you for coming."

Had they gazed into each other's eyes with the infinite longing of the young? How blue her face was, with its alien blotches of light. That sight he could remember clearly. The wheel had stopped turning and now they were standing on foreign earth again and facing each other in the silence where his heart beat. Had she put her face forward to be kissed? Had either he or she prolonged the conversation trying to think of something new to say while the magical silence lasted, the silence which was teeming with possibilities as a quiet loch with fish.

Where did you learn to shoot?

But all the time he was thinking something else. Should I dare or not? Should I kiss her? Have I the courage? Who are you, dear youth, whom I can hardly recall? Where have you gone? You are so clumsy, so hesitant, so pale. In your eyes there is an unfathomable hope, an innocence that will not return again. And you are standing there in the middle of the resonant silence. And if you kiss her perhaps that will change everything.

And he hadn't. He remembered that he had turned away, his feet making a rustling noise on the gravel just as, much later, they had done in the cemetery when his father had been buried and he with the others turned away. The sound of the gravel was life beginning again.

So he had left her without turning back, without waving, and he had heard a door closing gently behind him. And so he had walked home to his lodgings, to that house in which the old man—the landlady's father—still waited, with his sharp inquisitive ratlike face, and his little hostile grunt, as if he were a small Cerberus, waiting though not barking, just grunting feebly among the shadows.

And he had climbed the stairs and watched the moon through the windows of his attic room among the furniture which the spoilt cat sometimes scratched. He had lain on his back watching the moon with its terrifying scrutinizing eye moving stormily in and out of the clouds, creating coppery shapes, figures with ruffs hammered out of cloudy copper, faces, monstrous bodies, wings. Beautiful moon, how long you have existed, moon of lovers, staring paralysing moon whose relentless eye seems to see into the heart of men, moon which Perseus swings on his arm as if it were a stone on the end of a sling.

The bathroom chain was pulled and then there was silence. The old man had finally gone to bed and the house was at peace. The blue face hovered in front of his eyes, distinct, untouchable, and he turned over, his head on the cold white pillow, a nocturnal monk. But in the morning he had forgotten all about it, and had gone to classes as usual as if nothing had happened, and he had turned to his books again, even to Catullus, as if the fair had never existed, as if the Haunted House, the tunnel of lovers, no long existed. As if the blue face did not exist.

But it had existed. It had been another decisive moment in his life, a vision of reality which had faded as the blue light and the moon had faded. For he had not made any move, he had remained where he was, in the midst of his own existence.

He sensed a crowd of shades around him, and it seemed that they all had a definite destination in mind.

"Where . . ." he began but nobody listened to him, as they pushed past him while he stood there hesitantly with his case in his hand.

Eventually he was able to ask a small wrinkled man what was happening.

"It's Agamemnon and Achilles," he said. "Every Friday they have a slanging match. Each one stands on his own hill and then they shout across at each other."

"Every Friday," said Trill in amazement.

"That's right," said the small man. "That's what they do. It's what you might call a tradition."

Mr Trill followed him. Soon he found that a space of grass had been left vacant but that all round this area people were sitting or standing expectantly.

"Excuse me," he said continually, as he tried to force himself towards the front. But there was no need for him to be so anxious for on both sides of the space there were two gradually sloping hills, and as he watched he noticed that first from one side there came a warrior dressed in armour of complete black followed by his minions. Could this then be the great Achilles? He was tall and towering and his presence felt like death itself, huge and invincible. It was as if there poured from him deep dark rays of menace and power which drained the life from the spectators. He was still wearing his helmet, also black, and carrying at his side a huge spear.

From the other side there appeared another tall man but less tall than Achilles. His armour was bluish and his shield flashed and glittered in the dim light. His face also appeared commanding but not with the inner authority that blazed contemptuously from the eyes of Achilles, rather with a power that had been bestowed on him by others.

They came to a halt each on his own hill.

"Ha ha," said Achilles, "so she killed you when you didn't expect it."

And he laughed hugely while his minions echoed his laughter, some of them doubled over and slapping their knees.

"It's none of your business," said Agamemnon but looking embarrassed as if he had been caught in a shameful act.

"Well, you deserved it," said Achilles. "You were pretty useless as a commander anyway."

"I had to keep the army together and you were too temperamental to be of much help. You only helped when we were already winning."

"That's a lie," shouted Achilles angrily, "and you know it. But then you were always a liar. You were being beaten back to the ships when I came to your assistance. And did you not send a messenger to me pleading with me to come back?"

"I only did that because the army asked me to do so."

"Your army asked you! *Your* army!" said Achilles mockingly. "And if it hadn't been for your pettiness in taking my concubine away from me I would have fought from the very beginning. The trouble about you is that you can't handle men."

"And the trouble about you is that all you care about is your own vanity," shouted Agamemnon. "You only think about yourself. You the great 'star' who must be humoured like a child."

"Yes, and you spoke to me as if I was a child."

"So you were, a child."

"I wasn't a child. I was the one who killed Hector if you remember. I cut his head off and threw a dozen Trojans on the pyre to keep Patroclus company."

"That may be but you sulked like a girl for years while we bore the brunt of the fight. Wasn't it Ajax who was the great warrior in those days?"

"Ajax! You were glad enough to send me presents and my concubine back when you needed me and when Hector was causing havoc at the ships. You were frightened that you would lose the war and go back home with your tail between your legs. You the great commander! But it was I who saved you and don't you forget it."

"The fact is," said Agamemnon, "if Patroclus hadn't been killed you wouldn't have come out of your tent. He was your real concubine."

Achilles's terrible eyes seemed to dilate and his whole body in his black armour swelled with rage as he shouted.

"Why, you pathetic little man, if it wasn't for me you would have lost the war and you know it. The whole army knows it. What did you or your famous brother Menelaus do when Helen was stolen from him? No, it was left to me to save your reputation. You may look terrifying to others but not to me."

"My brother Menelaus fought as well as any man and later he enjoyed Helen when he took her back to Greece."

"And what about your own wife? Did you enjoy her? What about her lover who held a dagger behind his back for you as they unrolled the red carpet? Why you are nothing but a fool." And again the minions of Achilles laughed out loud clapping each other on the back and slapping their knees while the noise of their mockery was like that of a big stone rolling downhill.

"You may laugh," said Agamemnon, "but even you yourself had your weakness. You were not immortal as you thought you were. And after all what was your bravery but that which the goddess gave you?"

This thrust went down well with Agamemnon's followers who like those of the other side began to laugh immoderately. When Trill looked around him into the dimness he saw the spectators laughing too, some taking Agamemnon's side, some Achilles'. Their starved bored faces were twisted with hate and rancour.

"You were being cuckolded while you were away in the army wearing your campaign ribbons," shouted Achilles. "Your wife's lover served your wife as if she was a cow."

"It's hotting up now," said the small man with the bitter sharp eyes. "Now they'll go at each other."

"And what will happen then?" said Mr Trill.

"Nothing. They will just go back with their followers to where they were before. That's all."

"You mean that they don't fight," said Mr Trill.

"No. Not at all. Sh," said the small man impatiently.

"You compare me to a girl in a tent," said Achilles. "It's you who were the girl fighting for ten years for a woman's tits. A whore like all the others."

"And why then were you so fond of your own whore that you wouldn't fight because I took her away from you."

"*You* took her away from me! Why you streak of dog's spit I could have killed you if I'd wanted to. In the end it was only by a trick that you won the war."

"You were too stupid to think of a trick."

"I wasn't as stupid as you. Walking around the camp with your staff and your papers. You were always jealous of me. You didn't want another soldier in the army as great as yourself unless it was Ajax who was as stupid as you. And at the end you got what you deserved, you self-important staff officer. You and your brother were both tricked by women. Ha ha ha." And his laughter rolled like big stones among the phantom crowd.

"You are a laughing stock," he shouted. "Anyone who wears beautiful armour like you must be a laughing stock."

"And you didn't want to serve under anyone else, isn't that right?" said Agamemnon. "You didn't want to take the responsibility. You are nothing but a blockhead descended from a goddess as you say you are. Isn't that right?"

"No, it's not."

"Yes, it is."

"No, it's not."

"Yes, it is."

"No."

"Yes."

"No."

"Yes."

"Will they go on like this for a long time?" asked Mr Trill who was reminded of himself picking the petals of a flower in his youth and repeating the same monosyllables as these two great antique captains.

"Yes, they will go on like this till one of them gives up."

"And which one gives up?"

"I never wait to see."

"Do the others wait?"

"Some do, some don't."

"I see."

And Mr Trill got to his feet and wandered away till he could no longer hear the voices of the two soldiers. So this was what Achilles and Agamemnon had been like, shouting at each other like two bad-tempered boys.

What an extraordinary thing. Fighting each other over trivialities while the war raged around them. And yet perhaps that was how all wars were, life itself, even. He sat and thought about it for a long time. Was that really the substance of honour, fighting for the slightest thing, for a feather, for a rag of insult?

And all the time he had been thinking of them as two great invincible heroes who had fought for their country with complete dedication.

"No."

"Yes."

"No."

"Yes."

The words echoed back from his own childhood, from his schooldays, conkers on an autumn day.

He sighed heavily. What word, what picture, was now sacred, when all ideals were tumbling about him like a pack of cards.

He could hear the voice of his mother. "What are you doing reading those books all the time? Why can't you look around you? There's a garden to be done and the shed to be painted. But no, you spend all your time reading. Idleness, if you ask me."

And Mr Trill sat by himself in the dim shade, almost weeping, for it seemed to him that he had misspent his whole life, which had been a phantom one, far from the immediacies of the day. If only, he thought, if only I had enjoyed myself instead of locking myself away with my books. If only I had fought for my rights in the glare and heat of a life that after all only came once. His mother went out helmeted towards the street, to fight her little daily war against the headmaster's wife, who wouldn't speak to her. Her bony face thrust itself forward into the sunlight, and her knuckles whitened with rage, for the honour of the woman who had served in the canteen, with the scarf wound round her head like a flag among the dishes and the tables wet with tea and soup.

"O my God," thought Mr Trill putting his head in his hands.

"I think," said Mr Watt the new headmaster, the man whom Mr Trill called the Bingo Caesar, "that it would be a good idea if that boy Anderson were not to be given seven periods of your time for Greek this year. What do you say?"

He's only been here for six months, said Mr Trill to himself. I don't like him, and I think he's an inadequate fraud, not in any way to be compared with the great Roman headmasters we had before him, but nevertheless I must try to make things easier for him. After all he must feel this himself, that in scholarship, gentlemanliness, elegance of thought, he is inferior, and so I must help him.

"What do you suggest then, headmaster?" he asked him. What a comedian this man was, how could he ever have believed that he would fill the shoes of those who had gone before him and who had emerged from the Graeco-Roman world as civilized and liberal beings. Why, this man had emerged from the world of—Chemistry. He was large and bear-like, blunt and tactless, scholarship had not mellowed him nor made him humble. Perhaps his wife had pushed him to where he was now. Perhaps the undeviating road of ambition had showed him at last this post which was clearly too big for him.

"I suggest," said Watt, "that you take him along with your other class—the third year—and find room for him in that way."

But then Anderson was a real find. He had a feeling for poetry and, for his age, an unsurpassed knowledge of the classical world. He was a quiet well-behaved boy who absorbed with a relentless omnivorousness everything that Mr Trill could say to him. It was he for instance who in mathematics had learned about algebraic symbolism on his own and was reading Bertrand Russell at the age of fifteen.

Could he, Mr Trill, teach him while in his room there were thirty other pupils who had no feeling for Latin at all?

I must not let my dislike for the headmaster influence me in any way thought Mr Trill. His own ambition had never been excessive. In fact it was others who had made him apply for the post of Principal Teacher.

One day he had arrived in a room where there were about ten people, some men, some women, who glanced down at papers as he entered dressed in his best brown suit and brown tie. One woman had looked up at last and said,

"Do you think an unmarried man can have any knowledge of children?"

Mr Trill stared at her and then spoke the immortal words which had been part of his legend ever since.

"Madam, Vergil never married as far as we know, and he wrote the greatest poetry in the Latin language."

He heard someone—a man—snigger, and from that point there was no doubt that he would get the post.

"I'll take him with the third year," he said.

"Thank you very much, Mr Trill," said the headmaster and walked away whistling.

Later, in the staff-room, the young English master who made his pupils write poems about gangsters and cowboys remarked,

"I hear that our friend the headmaster is thinking of introducing our children to the industrial world. Princes of finance and bureaucrats from the town will talk to them once a week."

By this time Mr Trill was taking Anderson for Greek during the lunch periods in a little room up a poky little stair.

At the beginning of the following session, when he examined the brochure that the school published every year he noticed that Greek was no longer available.

"Why," he asked the headmaster, "is there no Greek this year?"

"It's quite simple, Mr Trill, there was only one pupil last year and I feel that it is not right to spend so much time on one pupil. Do you not agree with that yourself? Would it not be better for you to spend your undoubted talent on the less classical elements of the school? I have decided that the junior classes will be given classical studies instead. I suggest you introduce them to Rome and Greece, perhaps tell them something about the kinds of clothes they wore, cookery for the girls and sports for the boys. And so on."

He waved a vague hand and at that moment the telephone rang and Mr Watt, leaning back in his chair, spoke into it with great confidence while Mr Trill looked on.

Well, wasn't that right, thought Mr Trill to himself. Wasn't it right that as many as possible should be told something about the Roman and Greek world? It would mean however that he wouldn't be able to teach the poetry that he loved. Still, wasn't he being elitist and selfish in demanding that his own desires

should be satisfied? On the other hand he couldn't understand
what these lessons would be like. Was it simply a matter of filling
in blank periods for those who did not wish to have anything to
do with the classics in the first place?

Should he not really make a stand? But on the other hand how
undignified that would be. After all he despised Mr Watt and
the latter knew that. The question of the superiority of the
classics was not in doubt. And what were his arguments
anyway? Was he not simply admitting that he did not want the
"masses" to be educated in them. Mr Trill looked into Watt's
small eyes and at the centre of them he detected a little gleam of
hatred. Why was Mr Watt trying to destroy him? Was that what
lay behind his manoeuvrings? Why should Mr Watt hate him?
He had done nothing to him, in fact he had been very
accommodating. Did the headmaster despise his subject then?
Did he think that in the present day the classics were of no value?
The words flowed into the telephone. How smooth this Watt
appeared. Perhaps he, Mr Trill, should not have shown him any
sympathy at the beginning when he came to school first. The
walls were breaking, the barbarian was in charge.

"I . . ." he began, but Watt was waving him away, his hand
over the mouthpiece of the telephone, as if all had been settled.
Had it been settled then? Should he not return and debate every
inch of lost ground? From now on there would be no Greek in
the school and this meant that if any bright boy wished to study
Greek he would only be able to do it if Mr Trill tutored him in
his own time. Well, he could do that. Matters hadn't reached
such a pitch of greed and laziness that he couldn't do that. He
wasn't so interested in money that he would refuse a plea for
help. Mr Trill stood on the landing indecisively. Had he lost
another battle? Of course he had and he knew it. But on the
other hand those battles in the ditches were so undignified, so
impure. He didn't want to be another rat in the wainscoting.

Still . . . and he almost turned back, but he didn't.

How had Mr Watt become what he had now become, a
virtual dictator? And all the time, at least at the beginning, Mr
Trill had felt sorry for him, thinking that surely he must feel his

own inadequacy. But in fact he had been wrong. Mr Watt hadn't felt any inadequacy at all. He hadn't, in comparing himself with his predecessors, felt in any way inferior. How could that be, Mr Trill asked himself? It was so obvious that he was inferior, and yet he hadn't felt it. Was that because he was thick-skinned or because he actually was superior in some way?

"I don't understand what is happening," thought Mr Trill. The liberal classical world is collapsing around us, and *nobody notices*. What an extraordinary situation.

He stared at the wall on which someone had written GOEBBELS EATS HAGGIS. The light poured through the glass roof on to him. Where am I, he thought, what is this place supposed to be?

And yet . . . and yet . . . perhaps it is right that I should try and teach "the masses". And if I don't what can I say? Others, he knew, would be cunning enough to find a purely objective way of defending personal territory, but he wasn't clever enough to do that. His honesty was his weakness. He knew nothing about people. It was quite clear that he hadn't understood Mr Watt at any rate. It was obvious that the two of them belonged to two very different worlds. The small cunning eyes bored into his again.

I should really be defending my own territory, thought Mr Trill, and yet there is a certain amount of truth in what he is saying. It is perhaps wrong to give Anderson seven periods of Greek a week.

That had a truth in it but on the other hand was that the real reason why Mr Watt had stopped Greek? Mr Trill took another step down the stair and stopped again. Perhaps he should still go back. But what was he to say? No, it was no longer important that one should love one's subject, that was romantic idealism. What was important was to fight for everything you could get, find a quarrel in a straw. He took another step downstairs.

"You have been very accommodating," said Mr Watt later, "in fact I would say that you have been the most accommodating and most civilized of all the teachers that I have dealt with. So therefore it is with a certain amount of trepidation that"—he rested for a moment on the Latin word—"I approach you again." Was it Mr Trill's imagination or did Mr Watt use longer words usually derived from the Latin than he had done in the past? Why, once or twice recently, he had come to his room to ask him about the derivation of a word like "curriculum" and Mr Trill had been glad to expatiate, despising himself at the same time for basking in the warm glow of power.

"Well then," said Mr Watt, "you will have heard of my plans for talks to be given by professional local people on selected topics, for example the law, medicine and so on. The question arises about a room for them." And he glanced round Mr Trill's large and airy room and at his small class.

"I was wondering whether you would be willing that they use this room during these periods. This would only occur once or twice a week. And you could have Mr Blake's room at that time. Mr Blake is free. He has a small Chemistry room as you will know."

I know what he is doing, thought Mr Trill. Eventually he will get this room entirely for Mr Blake, or entirely for these industrial and professional conferences and I will be teaching in Mr Blake's poky room till the end of my days. I know that this is exactly what he is doing. But what shall I say? Shall I say that he can find another room for his conferences, in which case he will tell me that there is no other room more suitable. Or shall I say that I am against these conferences in the first place? But how can you be, he will say. After all, these poor children cannot go out into the world blind and deaf.

And in any case, thought Mr Trill, does it matter where I teach Latin? Do I need a sunny room such as this one is and which I have inhabited for twenty years and which I love? Is this not selfishness on my part? Why, is my comfort to be more important than the future lives of the children as they set out on their journey through life?

"I don't mind," he said. And again the small sharp eyes glittered with their lights of sharp hate, if that was what it was.

Who are you, thought Mr Trill, who are you really? My scholarship after all is no use to me in this world. All this time you weren't weak at all, all this time when I felt pity for you you knew exactly what you were doing. All this time when I wept for you because you were such a pigmy you thought of yourself as a giant. And perhaps you have gone home and discussed me with your wife and she has helped you to find my weakest spot, just like Achilles. How can I stand out against you, against these ratlike movements, with my shaken armour?

And so without argument Mr Trill surrendered more and more, till finally he had hardly anything at all left. Dressed in his dignity he found that dignity didn't count at all. The past was forever gone and only the present remained and the present was fashioned by these devious manoeuvrings.

Perhaps then he should have fought from the very beginning for every piece of chalk in his room, for every jotter, every desk. Perhaps that was what fighting and honour really meant.

And his father, by retreating into his study, had been wrong, and his mother by intuition had been right all along.

Hail to the Bingo Caesar, he shouted among the shades. And he raised an imaginary glass.

From a deep shade behind him he thought he heard the sound of weeping and there under a tree he saw a woman who was dressed in black. Above her flowed the dark distraught leaves.

"Who are you?" he asked.

"Andromache," she replied.

"The wife of Hector?" he asked.

"The same," she said.

"Why then are you weeping?"

"It is because of my fear," she said.

"Fear of what?" asked Mr Trill.

"Not fear of death," she replied. "Not fear of death but another fear. A greater fear than that."

"What fear is that?"

"Fear of loss," said the woman as she shivered uncontrollably under the shadow of the leaves.

"Everyone knows," she began, "what happened to my husband Hector. Everyone knows that he had to go out to fight

Achilles. I remember it very well. I helped him put on his armour on that never-to-be-forgotten day. He was trembling with fear but when I asked him whether he should still go out, he said,

" 'I must, I must,' over and over. I asked him why he should go out when he was frightened but he kept saying, 'I must, I must,' like a little child. That day was a day of sorrows. It was a beautiful calm blue day and the soldiers were gathered together to watch the fight for they themselves wouldn't have to take part. And my husband Hector put on his armour on that calm blue day with the mist in the air and I said to him, 'Why do you have to go out and fight?' and he kept saying, 'I must, I must.' His mother Hecuba was there and his father Priam and to them he returned the same answer.

"And you know what happened to him. In spite of the fact that he ran round the walls of Troy to escape the terrible Achilles and finally had to turn and fight he was still carried about the dust of the plain tied to the victor's chariot wheels." And she began to weep uncontrollably. "And you know how Priam had to beg for my husband's body in order that it might be buried. And Achilles threw the bodies of many Trojans on to the same pyre as that of Patroclus. But that was not it. That was not what I was talking about. For there was much else that no one knows about."

There was a long silence and it seemed to Mr Trill that she would not speak again but at last she said very slowly and quietly.

"Men do not know what women suffer. None of them knows that. For if they must go out and fight we must stay where we are. We must look after the children and we must knit and tidy and clean. The house or the castle must be kept, whether we know or not that the war will soon be lost and we ourselves will be taken prisoner or raped. Thus it was that while Hector fought I must keep the house together, and Priam and Hecuba were old.

"But it was not even that. It was worse than that, much worse. All day Helen went about the castle, young and beautiful, gazing into her mirror as if she were a girl. She was the

centre of the world's attention, men fought over her. How could
she not be happy? How could she not look on herself as valuable
and important? Every day she would wake up in the morning
and how could she not say to herself, 'I am the centre of the
whole world. Great armies are dying and fighting all the time
because of me.' On the other hand, I worried about my husband
continually while I must give orders to the servants to keep the
affairs of the palace running smoothly. And who was to say to me
that the two great armies were fighting over me? No one was to
say that, no one. Every woman must be encouraged and told
that she is beautiful. But how could Hector do that when he was
out fighting every day? When he was taking the responsibility
for a whole kingdom? And all the time Helen was singing and
dancing and happy in the house, for she knew that if the Trojans
lost Menelaus would take her back again. All she had to do was
keep herself beautiful for any eventuality, while I on the other
hand lost my beauty every day because of the responsibility I
was enduring. No one can know the anger and the rancour that I
felt. Because of her my husband was going out to die, because of
her my father and mother were trembling with fear, because of
her Trojans were dying every day, and all she could do was sing
and keep herself beautiful.

"One day I lost control of myself and I told her all this. And
who took her side? I will tell you. It was Hector. One day I said
to her, 'Why don't you go and give yourself to Menelaus, and
the Greeks can go home?' But she only looked up from her
mirror and smiled for though she was beautiful she was stupid. I
could have torn her eyes out. I could have scratched her face to
make her less lovely than she was. But who was it who stopped
me? It was Hector, my own husband. It was the same Hector
who must go and die for her, for a girl – I cannot even call her a
woman – who didn't care. What was it to her that I would be
without a husband? She had seen many husbands die and one
more wouldn't make any difference. And as she was the most
beautiful girl in the world so Hector was the greatest soldier.
And he loved her. O I know that he loved her. He told me that
he didn't, he insisted that he didn't, but I knew that he did. A

woman cannot be deceived. He saw me as old and wrinkled, and
he saw her in the dew and blossom of her youth. How could he
not love her? I have no proof that he slept with her, that I do not
know. But I do know that he loved her. When he didn't think
that I was looking at him, his eyes would follow her about the
palace and she would walk with her swaying woman's walk. I
knew what she was doing but Hector did not know. One night I
accused him of being in love with her. I said that if he wished to
leave me he could do so. If he thought me old he should find
someone younger. 'I am not keeping you back,' I told him. For I
was insane with jealousy. And why should I not be? I knew that
he loved her though he refused to admit this to himself, and yet
he was going out to die for her, leaving me alone to take all the
responsibility. Who would blame me for my jealousy?

"I remember the morning he left and went out of the gate of
the palace for the last time. Though he was trembling he looked
heroic. The palace and the people depended on him. He knew
that and everyone knew it. Only Priam and Hecuba and I were
sure that he would not live, for who could survive an encounter
with Achilles? His armour suited him, he looked handsome and
radiant. Only I was aware of the fact that he had been
trembling, for of course being his wife I knew everything. And
then as he was leaving he kissed us all. He kissed me first and
then Hecuba and Helen. Lightly, as it seemed to me, on the lip
as if she were his sister. But that was only what he wished us all to
think. I on the other hand knew that the kiss was a more
meaningful one than that. I knew that she was the only one
among us whom he would have wished to kiss with passion
though he restrained himself. I knew that it was she alone whom
he loved. And she too realized it and turned to me with her
blazing triumphant eyes and at that moment I could have killed
her. But being who I was I had to remain silent. I had to preserve
my dignity to the end as Hector had to preserve his courage, the
image of the great soldier and hero, even though he was going to
his death and knew it. Never have I suffered so much in my life
before or since, seeing my husband setting out to fight a great
soldier and a god, for a woman younger and more beautiful than

me, and knowing that he was setting out with a lie in his heart. How beautiful that day was, how blue, how calm, and how terrible was the beating of my heart. It was Helen who waved gaily to him as he turned for the last time with his puzzled face and his brow which I knew would be wrinkling under his helmet.

"My love my love I cried to him. And then I heard the scream, like the scream of an animal in agony, and when I turned and looked it was as if Helen was trembling with ecstasy as she might have done in the marriage bed. Her eyes were large and very clear and yet at the same time turned inwards on themselves and her lips were large and full and soft and her whole body was trembling as if at the height of love. I cannot tell you what I felt at that moment for I knew that she was an animal in heat and that she wished to go out and give herself to the victor Achilles in the prime of his courage and his triumph.

"I could have slapped her face, I could have bitten her ear off, but in spite of all my rage, I had to maintain my dignity, for there was much to be done, Priam and Hecuba to be looked after, and my child to be pacified. I could have turned into a stone that morning but I didn't.

"I could have dropped down dead where I was, but I could not afford even that, there was too much to do.

"And that is what broke my heart, that Hector loved Helen and he had gone out from me with a lie in his heart. Perhaps he had never slept with her but nevertheless the lie was in his mind. His love had passed from me to her, from age to youth."

She became silent under the shadow of the leaves and Mr Trill felt a desolation in his heart as if it had been pierced. He wanted to say something but there was nothing that he could say. All he could do was bow his head in front of that suffering, while the woman's silence swelled and swelled as if it would overwhelm him totally. And there together they sat in the dark shade of the trees, each thinking his thoughts till finally with a deep sigh the woman rose and left him.

At the age of thirty-four Mr Trill had fallen in love with one of his pupils, a girl called Thelma who had long blond hair worn in a pigtail. At first Mr Trill did not know that he was in love for he had never been in love before. It was only when he realized that he was extremely sad when Thelma was absent from his class that he finally knew that he was in love. The only problem was that Thelma was at the most seventeen. Mr Trill began to re-read Catullus in his room at night but could find in that famous Latin poet only salacity and not the pure true language that he craved. For his love was agonizingly sweet and weighted with youth and mortality. It was as if Thelma's youth, its imagined pains and terrors and exquisite joys, was a sign of eternity that concerned itself only with the soul.

As he bent over her jotter to see how she had translated a passage from Livy that he had set, it seemed to him that a faint perfume wafted from her that did not belong to her as such but to a kingdom of which she was simply an emanation. And this was especially so on summer mornings when the mist had not yet been dispersed, and he saw her enter the room in her blue blazer and skirt as if she were not a woman at all, but the spirit of eternal youth, a youth that had forever passed from Mr Trill and which he could hardly remember.

In all the time however that Mr Trill was in love with Thelma he in no way made any advances to her since to him youth was sacred, and especially so as he was a teacher. Thus he sighed in secret and his heart bled in private. At night when he lay in bed he thought of Thelma as of some unattainable star which shone straight into his bedroom from unimaginable distances, a kind of Diana, a huntress connected with spring woods and delicate waters.

How happy Mr Trill was in those days and how well, in his opinion, he taught. It was as if he was inspired and his happiness in the presence of Thelma reflected on to her fortunate class. She was the daughter of a man who worked in the local agricultural office, though Mr Trill of course could not believe this. She was no more his daughter than she was Persephone. She was flesh and blood but she was more than that. Her perfume was that of the Muses as they disported themselves around Helicon.

He found ways of lending her books which in fact she did not read—books with titles like *The Greek Mind* or *The Thought of Greece*—but she was not interested in the classics, and her brightness was not in any case exceptional. Nevertheless Mr Trill saw signs in her exercises of a budding brilliance. In her presence words like "mensa" and "insula" had a music of their own, and, once gaunt and antique, became vernal and tender. Sometimes he would sit on his tall barren chair wondering how he could get through the day without seeing her again.

At times he would dream that he might some day marry her, but these times occurred only rarely for to him she was not a being of flesh and blood such that he could imagine her as a wife, whatever that might be like, but as an inspiration and guide through the banality of the days, a sort of Beatrice. If only she would remain as she always was, in that breathless moment when beauty is poised at its height before it begins to tremble and waver and finally fall like a dewdrop from a branch in the early morning when the gossamer webs are drifting in the breeze.

Not a sign however did Thelma give that she loved him in return or was at all occupied with these omens and portents of eternity. Not a sign did she give that his scholarship was devoted to her, that all he was and all he possessed he was willing to lay in a moment at her feet. If Mr Trill had been in the habit of going to school dances he would have attended them for her sake alone but he could not bring himself to do that, for his mirror, as he thought, taught him his unworthiness. Why, he had seen too much of the world for her to love him. He was soiled with knowledge and irony and rancour. And he was too old for her.

He existed in what only could be called a mist of love since his love had no reality in the world around him, was not anchored in it, and could not issue in any fruition. If she was spring he was autumn, and if she had suddenly said to him at some moment charged with significance that she was his forever he would probably have run away, his gown floating behind him. For he craved the pure and impossible which he saw only in her.

Not that some of the other pupils were not sharp-eyed and malicious enough to see what was happening. They all said that old Trill was in love with Thelma and teased her with their knowledge. And Thelma was in one way proud and in another embarrassed. For it could not be said that Mr Trill was handsome nor that his teaching though enthusiastic was interesting. Her own interests were in romantic books and horoscopes. Mr Trill, whose knowledge of classics was devoted and pure, would have been horrified if he had known the quality of the magazines that she devoured every weekend and how firmly she believed that the stars controlled her every action. If in fact she had been in love with Mr Trill she would have searched her horoscopes for signs and omens, she would have asked her aunt to read her tea leaves for her, she would have seen the whole world as an open book trembling with apparitions. The slightest action such as breaking a cup would have been prodigal of supernatural signals and her diary would have been as important to her as Vergil was to him. But Mr Trill remained in ignorance of that world of possible commotions and storms, pullings of hair and jealousies, for to Mr Trill the universe was an ordered place which now and again throbbed with lines from the great poets who had never felt in their whole lives despairs and terrors but had been inspired to their highest flights by the gods themselves.

Was it perhaps that Mr Trill, sensing that his youth was leaving him, committed all his feelings to that one girl representative to him of all youth, or was it that he was truly in love? Who can tell? It is certain that if she had been ill he would have been able—if he had been asked—to wait patiently at her bedside for hours and days on end. But as for her days of health what could he do during them? She was certainly pretty with her fair pigtail, her pale face with very blue eyes, her long slender neck, her blue blazer and her blue skirt. She was like a ship that is ready to leave harbour and enter the mist that shrouds all youth when it sets off on its journey. How he would have protected her in his imagination from that hollow journey from which he could see great suffering and difficulties springing, similar in fact to the ones that he had endured himself.

If he had only known her as she really was, her hurried glances at unfinished homework, her concern with hockey, her wish that one day she would have a pretty house, nice clothes and crystal vases, and her total attention to the banalities emitted by disc jockeys in the early hours of the morning before she went to school. If he had only seen her mind that was totally ordinary, and realized that never once did she think of Vergil after she had finished her set work for the day and that she panicked totally when she was faced by a difficult problem in Matthematics. If he had seen her when she was dressing for a school dance pirouetting in front of the long mirror in the corridor. If he had seen her when she was quarrelling with her younger brother at breakfast every morning while she grabbed at the last minute the thin slice of toast that was her only sustenance at that time of day since she was looking after her figure. If he had seen her mind which was a storehouse of miscellaneous information and feelings, like an antique shop which is cluttered with all sorts of goods leaning crazily against each other, mirrors, mattresses, wardrobes, pillows and hundreds of other articles which have settled there as naturally as snow.

But he did not see this, he only saw her in his classroom when the sun shone through the window on to her hair, making it radiant and pure, flawless and perfect. If he had seen the treachery of which she was capable, the tantrums, the jealousies, but, no, he saw none of these.

Sometimes he tried to catch her eye, but she always looked away. Was it perhaps that she had not seen him? Was it that she was dreaming some impossible dream of youth? Was it, dreadful thought, that she did not really like him? But at least he could test that by marking her jotter, by being close to her, by, most daring action of all, sitting beside her in the same desk.

And soon she would be leaving the school altogether, soon she would be setting out on her temporal voyage after her eternity of dreaming, and he would never see her again. The days were passing and the end of the session was approaching. How his heart beat as if it wished to squeeze a value out of every passing moment. Soon the last bell would toll and she would walk out of the gates with her school bag over her shoulder, over her arm, among all the other ex-prefects and ordinary scholars. Soon she would enter the summer after her spring. And for these months, these weeks, these days, the desks glittered as if with a supernatural radiance, and Mr Trill spent himself on poetry and rhetoric. The days passed, the bells rang, the hours were devoured. Soon the school would be a dark place again without illumination. My youth, my youth, is going, thought Mr Trill.

And then one fatal day he passed by design the room which the senior girls were allowed to use during their free time. Perhaps he thought that he would catch a glimpse of her whom he loved through the half-open door. In front of him he could see the cracked mirror in which the girls studied their own reflections, and there standing in front of it was another girl, not Thelma, but someone else. Who? What was her name? Muriel? And Muriel, with coat flying about her as if it were a gown was parading in front of the mirror and saying,

"And now Thelma my dearest love, *carus cara carum*, will you please tell me what Vergil meant by these famous words which he once spoke when having a solitary pee in Italy. Will you please tell me that, my dearest Thelma?"

He couldn't see her face in the mirror because the glass was cracked and she for the same reason could not see him. Her capped head flashed and flickered, and her gown swung and floated. And from behind her, though he could see no one, he heard the happy clear laughter of Thelma, as if she were delighted with the performance which spotty-faced Muriel was giving. He stood transfixed. He . . . He could not go in, he would not give them that pleasure, he was too proud, too dignified for that. But if ever a heart . . . if ever a heart was broken it was his. Dazed he stood, the pain piercing his soul, and listened to the happy laughter as if it were coming to him from the depths of hell itself, from that inferno in which Vergil and Dante had travelled. His legs shook, his face was on fire. What a fool he had been, what an old fool. To think that he had ever credited that girl with any delicacy of feeling, to think that he had thought she would walk with him through these shining pages, so resonant with power and pathos. No, it was impossible. Never again, never, never again. Never again would he give his heart to anyone in order to endure such mockery. Muriel disported herself in front of the cracked mirror of that poky room and there just outside it, a frail eavesdropper, Mr Trill died.

And thus it was that when the pupils came to say goodbye to him he wasn't available: he had as he had written on the board been asked to take part in an urgent meeting. In fact he was standing alone in the library watching them leave the school for the last time, now and again turning back to look, and waving their scarves in the air, as they entered the street on which people talked and walked, and passed the shops in which the transactions of the world were carried out. Mr Trill hardened his heart forever and put on his Roman shield, while at the same time he read that poem of Catullus in which he says goodbye to his brother and which ends,

Et in perpetuum, frater, ave atque vale.

In his wanderings, still carrying his case as if he were a clerk in a dimly lit office, Mr Trill had come to the banks of the river again but at a different point from that at which he had landed. It flowed sluggishly along through the pervading mist and beyond it Mr Trill could see the vague mass of the castle about which he had previously been told. It seemed to him that he could hear from the thin mist the baying of hounds.

"Strange," said a voice from behind him and when Mr Trill turned round in a startled manner he saw a little man with a wrinkled puzzled brow who was gazing at him with dull eyes.

"No one knows what goes on in there," said the man. "I've often stood here and wondered. Some people go into that castle and they never come out again. I've seen it happening." And he nodded his head wisely two or three times.

"That's odd," said Mr Trill.

"It is indeed," said the little man speaking rapidly like one who wishes to convince his audience of an important idea.

"I have a natural turn of curiosity myself, my wife often used to speak to me about it, and I have often stood here wondering what is going on over there. I have seen people being ferried across to the castle and for a moment when they land the hounds seem to stop barking and there is silence but the people never come back. Not once have I seen any of them returning."

Mr Trill found it hard to place the man's accent: it was as if he was pretending to be more educated than he really was. His mind, attracted by puzzles—every morning in the staff-room he had been in the habit of filling in a newspaper crossword—brooded vaguely on the castle. Was there some secret connected with it? Did some terrible fate belong to it, some obscene tortures? Was there even in Hades a group of people who managed the shadowy territory as if it were a real empire.

And if so who were these people and why were they never seen?

"Some people say," said the little man as if he had understood Mr Trill's thought, "that men's brains are taken out of their heads and stored in the cellars there."

"Oh," said Mr Trill shivering.

"But most of us just want to stay here," said the little man sadly. "We suffered enough while we were on earth."

"That's true," said Mr Trill. "I can understand that and one could be happy enough in this place—even in this place."

"Yes, indeed," said the little man. "However, perhaps you are different. Perhaps you are an adventurer and wish to see what is going on on the other side."

"Not me," said Mr Trill. "I have suffered enough too and in any case there is more than enough here to puzzle me without looking for more."

"Every man to his nature," said the little man. "For myself I have always been of an inquisitive nature and I spend a lot of my time here on the bank of the river thinking and wondering what is happening in the castle. But that is the way I am," he said proudly. "Not everyone is like that."

He brooded for a moment and continued, "Anyway, I'm not important. I was never important. There were millions like me when I was alive. But I always had this curiosity. When my fellow workmen were content to accept orders I would wonder if they were the right orders, do you understand me, and why they were being given. And many times I thought I could have done a better job myself."

"I can appreciate that," said Mr Trill absently.

"You are saying that but you are not listening to me much," said the little man in a resigned voice. "I understand that and I'm used to it. No one ever listened to me. I used to sit and people would talk around me and it was as if I wasn't there. This place now is full of gods and goddesses. But have you ever thought how hard it is for people like me to get up in the morning?" And he fixed Mr Trill with his dull eyes. "There is nothing ahead of them, no glory, nothing like that. All they have is their work. Famous people have great events to look forward to. They have parties, and they get invited to dinners, but nothing like that ever happened to me. Our wives despise us because nothing important happens to them through us. And women like to be noticed, they like to dress up, to speak to important people."

As he spoke the man seemed to become smaller and smaller, almost diminishing to the size of a dwarf, and Mr Trill thought that even his colour was changing as if from white to brown or even black. His brow too was wreathed with wrinkles which looked like tiny snakes.

"I can tell that you once were a man of importance," said the little man. "It's in the way you walk, the way you speak. But I never had any power. Sometimes when the day was stormy I didn't want to get up from my bed. I had to force myself to put my feet on the floor. My sons and daughters despised me, for I wasn't famous in any way. No one saluted me when I passed them on the street. In shops I was served last because even the shop assistants knew that I wasn't important. And if I tried to kick up a row they wouldn't listen to me, they ignored me as if I wasn't there. And sometimes I could hardly hear my own voice. Policemen pushed me aside and charged me with offences because I had no one to protect me. They would rough me up and then let me free and not even apologize. That happened to me once, it was a case of mistaken identity but the cops just said, 'Don't you show your face here again, you little bastard.' 'And what about my scars,' I said, 'what about my black eye.' 'Your black arse more like. Clear off or we'll mark you for life.' But of course they don't do that, they use rubber truncheons so they don't mark you. Why, even my wife didn't meet me off the ferry because she was ashamed of me. No one loved me all the days of my life. Can you understand what I'm telling you?" said the little man, who had almost become a hunchback in the dim light. "All I saw of the world was my bench and my tools. And if I had an idea someone else would take the credit for it. Oh, they spoke nice to you but they took the credit just the same. If I told a joke I always got the story wrong because of nervousness and no one could get the point of it. I was always flustered and I spoke too fast and so no one bothered with me. Even you aren't listening to me properly. You are saying to yourself, Why doesn't this fellow stop speaking? What is he on about? But I have thoughts of my own too and I'm not stupid. I was a good carpenter in my day, I have my certificate. There are a lot of the young ones now who don't have a certificate and couldn't care less, but I cared. I liked to make a piece of good furniture. Understand me? Are you listening? I took pride in my work but the others don't do that. Why I've seen them putting nails, would you believe it, in mahogany instead of joints. And have you seen their tables and their chairs? A dog wouldn't sit on them. And they talk and people listen to them, that's what I can't understand. They don't care about anything but they are listened to just the same. Even my wife didn't listen to me. Perhaps you've never had that experience. Perhaps you were never married. You don't look as if you were married. Oh, I notice things and I said to myself, as soon as I saw you, I don't think this fellow is married.

"Even my children laughed at me and because I was so small they would beat me up to get money for the gambling machines. When they grew up and were earning a wage they never gave me any of it; they would say, We didn't ask to be born. They expected their food and lodging as if they had a right to it. And what about me I used to say to them, Do you think I wasn't born? They blamed me for their lives, for bringing them into the world. I was tortured by them, they made fun of me, they imitated me.

"My children and my wife despised me. What was there for me? Many a time I thought of killing myself but the good God has told us not to do that. And anyway I never had the courage. Do you know what the difference between the rich and the poor is? I've thought about it a lot and even more since I came here. The rich have a future, do you understand me, and the poor don't have a future. There was a star I used to watch in the sky in the morning before I went to work. It might have been Venus, I don't know. It was as sharp as a thorn. I used to hate that star and yet I looked for it every morning when I got out of my bed.

"Even when I died my family scrambled for the few things that I had. Do you know that they broke the joint of my finger to get my ring. See, I can show it to you."

And he showed Mr Trill his broken finger as if it were a trophy. "And they bought the cheapest coffin they could find. I knew about good wood and I knew it was cheap. But they didn't care. And how many were at my funeral? I can tell you. Six. My wife didn't come. She pretended she was too sick. Imagine that.

"Every day that passed was like every other day, except that some days if I had nerve enough I got drunk. But then my wife would shout and scream at me and say to me, How do you expect me to pay for the hairdresser if you're going to be as drunk as a pig? You tell me that. She was like a knife in my side. She didn't just want food and shelter. She wanted honour, she wanted people to look up to her. Why did I live at all, that is what I wish to ask."

And the small man gazed up at Mr Trill with the large liquid eyes of a dog and Mr Trill could find no answer to his question.

"I thought so," said the little man, "I thought so. I don't blame you. I don't blame you at all. I don't blame anyone at all. This is how it is."

And before Mr Trill could speak he had faded into the mist so that after a moment it was as if he had never been there at all, as if he were only an emanation of the mist, while behind him the castle glowered in the dimness, the castle whose purpose was obscure, and from whose environs hounds howled now and

again, as if they themselves were questioning, with their wet
snouts, the mist around them.

There was a blind blundering about him and Mr Trill recoiled
as a gigantic figure loomed out of the mist, like a wrecked yet
moving ship.

"Aargh," said the mouth of the figure, and its words were
strangled in its throat.

"I," said Mr Trill about to run still clutching his case. "I . . ."

"Aargh," said the figure searching for him and laying a hand
on his arm. The massive head leaned down towards him, in the
middle of it a scorched single dead eye, piteously dead.

It was like the huge idiot that Mr Trill had often seen, in the
town where he taught, in his vast flapping coat standing in the
middle of the road and directing the traffic while sometimes the
policemen looked on benevolently and sometimes drew him
kindly away on to the safe pavement.

"You?" said the figure, lightly touching his arm.

"Mr Trill," said Mr Trill in an agitated voice.

"Trill," echoed the huge mouth. "Trill."

The word was like a big stone in its jaw.

"Noman?" said the figure, "No man?"

"No," said Mr Trill, "not no man." Surely this giant was not
still searching for the nimble Ulysses even in the depths of
Hades. "Not Noman," said Mr Trill thinking of the painting
by Turner where Ulysses stood high on his ship, his arms spread
triumphantly in victory while he waved his flag and around the
ship sailors like dead souls milled, and on the left there was the
darkness which the raw sun had not yet illuminated.

"Noman," said the figure with a sigh. "Alone was. Noman
came, killed my sheep, killed my good sheep, ate them. Lucky I
caught. Ate them."

"What?" said Mr Trill, "did Noman eat your sheep? Was
that why you . . . ?"

"Alone was, shepherd, harming noman. My lovely sheep. Ate
them."

"But," said Mr Trill, "that is not . . ."

"Got them. . . . Ate." The giant licked his lips as if he felt blood on them.

"Cheated me. Said name Noman." His dead eye turned towards Trill, a waste circle.

And Mr Trill had a vision. Inside the cave the quick intelligence of Ulysses searched lithely, seized on the stick, grew an eye, liquid, smart, Mediterranean, put out the other savage eye, and blazed afresh as with the sharp vision of a fierce dedication to survival.

It was the new blue eye of the Mediterranean, European, scientific, piercing, single, egotistical.

"My sheep, lovely sheep," said the pastoral giant. "Killed them. Noman spoke. Lonely. His voice echoed."

The massive hands had left Mr Trill's arm and they flapped about in the mist like grey claws, extinct, searching.

"Felt for them. Threw stones. Heard them falling in the water. Laughed at me." He stopped as if he were listening to the laughter coming out of the darkness, echoing from all directions. "Noman, noman, noman," said the laughter. And that was what it was, thought Mr Trill, it was the laughter of Noman, the new Noman, the interchangeable Noman, the schemer who would survive, the nameless one, eternal salesman of the new moving world. Where Noman went no flowers grew but around the ancient giant there was a solid shadow, a place of ancient songs and foliage.

"Noman," said the mouth. "Talker. Little man. Mouth always going. Speaking. Took sheep away."

The long sharp stick hissed through his eye and he was blundering about on the headland where the wind howled, the wind of his own land, dear to him, now blind, unseen. The sound of the wind was like the music of strings, singing about the lonely land, while Ulysses headed for the cities, devious, a blue eel.

"Noman," sighed the giant. "Cheated me. Caught him eating sheep. Ate the little men. Eye put out. Alone. Shouted No man. Noman came. Noman didn't come." He floundered about in the dead branches of language, puzzled, blundering. "Noman didn't come, went on in ship. Noman came, of own people. Laughed. All laughed. Noman laughed. Every man laughed. Own people laughed. Brothers, sisters laughed. Noman laughed, laughter everywhere."

And Mr Trill heard the laughter coming from all directions, thousands and thousands of little distinct laughters blending into one huge laughter as if like the sun on the Mediterranean the world was a bowl of sunny laughter. And through it moved Ulysses, a thin whip of survival, heading for his island, his mind ticking ceaselessly like a bomb, an infection returning home.

Laughter everywhere, the ironic laughter of the whole world, echoing Noman, the sea and the rocks laughing, as little Noman flourished his flag and the sails filled, and the sea waited, laughing ceaselessly. In the centre of the laughter was little vain Noman on whom the joke was as much as on the stranded giant, lost among his vast woolly sheep.

"Alone was," said the giant with the words like pebbles in his throat. "Night and day the same. Eye bandaged, people about me. Who? they said. Noman, I said. And they laughed. Eye throbbed. Pain everywhere. In plain, on hills. Nothing seen."

Tenderly Mr Trill touched the giant's arm. The monster sighed as if pleased. His vast blind head nodded in the air above, searching.

Mr Trill saw them all in their tribes, in the caves, huddled together, their sheep about them. The sun rose, the sun set, day after day: darkness came down, darkness dispersed. The fields were white, then black. Still they huddled together, rose in the morning, then tended their sheep.

Then Noman came. The island was seen by a new eye, a quick moving eye that investigated advantages, positions, vegetation, food. It moved about the island seeking to use it, falling now here, now there, like a torch, powerful and shining. It did not hear the music of the island, the antique tune that the wind made, had made for century after century. It was a famished restless eye that would not cease moving till death came. It did not see the antique heavy settled figures.

Noman was a stranger on the island, but it was as if it belonged to him, as if its politics were his, as if its future belonged to him. The sharp unjaded salesman seized on all things on the island as a woman picks up and adores her own dear ornaments, which are hers alone, which tell who she is. It is her house, every corner, every cranny, every little china figure. So the island was to Noman, for Noman was no man. He was the little figure lost in eternity but determined that eternity should echo with his mind.

"Noman," came the voice out of the mist. And the huge stones fell into the water and beside the boat there was the thick darkness that not even Noman could illuminate. Though the rigging might hum, the darkness would always follow the ship like a stain, and no sunlight would ever darken it.

"Sorry," said Mr Trill over and over.

"Name Sorry?" said the giant.

"No, name Trill, but sorry sorry."

The giant gazed blankly down, among the thickets of language, a lost head. It sighed as if the words were painful to it, like the stick that it remembered, the sharp burning stick that hissed about its once serene ring.

"Sorry, sorry," said Mr Trill, "most sorry."

The craggy head lowered and sighed among the mist.

"It is Noman that caused it," thought Mr Trill. And it seemed to him that he had been given a tremendous revelation, so huge that he could hardly grasp it, as he could not grasp the grey giant who was so helpless beside him. The physical was manoeuvred by the mental, the body was guided by the mind. The headlands, ancient with music, surrendered to the intelligence. Ulysses was the blue sharp quick Mediterranean eel.

"Alone," said the giant. And its voice echoed in the greyness. "Alone."

It bent its head down over Mr Trill as if seeking, and then with the same sigh, as if it had smelt from him, as well, the betrayals of civilization, turned away, and blundered off like a big sad dog into the mist.

Mr Trill stood behind the lectern and made his last speech.

"There have been many changes since I came to this school. I would like to think that in the early days the influence of the

Roman and Greek traditions was very strong but now all that has gone. In the old days we wore gowns but now hardly anyone wears a gown. I remember Mr Mason who taught History. He used to mark three hundred exercises a week. He was a man devoted to his studies, a true Roman. Sometimes I think that it wasn't Octavius who won at all but Mark Antony and that he brought Cleopatra to Rome: but I have only thought this in more recent times.

"I have been very happy here on the whole. My greatest delight was when some pupil or other came to me and asked me the meaning of the words in a poem, but that, I regret to say, was in my early career. However all is not yet lost and we pass the torch on to the young who will, we hope, keep it alight. As I stand here behind this lectern I feel I am only saying *au revoir*, not goodbye. The dead are always with us though we may sometimes forget that. A School is not a building, it is a communion of the living and the dead. Have we not added our tiny stone to the cairn that is perpetually being built? My father was a classics master as I am and he passed down his tradition to me. My mother . . ." And here Mr Trill paused but didn't finish the sentence.

"I know that on days like these it is traditionally the case that we tell jokes. But I feel in too sombre a mood to tell jokes. For I see every day the barbarians approaching more and more closely to the walls." And here he looked directly into the eyes of the headmaster. "I see our traditions dying, discipline being eroded day after day. Is it our fault? Is it the fault of society? Who knows? Is it the treason of the clerks? I remember when I came here first the headmaster told me,

" 'You must never sit down when you are teaching. How can a man teach well when he is sitting down?' I have never forgotten his words and I have always obeyed them. For when you sit down you begin to grow lazy, and laziness is our enemy. Laziness and despair. I have never despaired. In spite of everything I have always kept in front of me the example of the Romans, people like Brutus and Cato. For how can we live unless we have great exemplars to sustain us?

"I remember many years ago there was a boy in this school and he couldn't pass his Latin which he needed for getting into university. I spent my intervals and free periods teaching him. And he managed to pass after all, he managed to get into university. But what did he do when he got there? He started to drink and go out at nights instead of attending to his studies and the next I heard of him he was working as a conductor on the buses. At times like these one feels that there is no point in going on. But there *is* a point in going on. It is a struggle which must be renewed every day, and we must not fail the generations, though it is true it seems to me that the earlier generations were the most mature and the most hardworking. There is a responsibility on us all, that is why we become teachers in the first place. I could never imagine myself as other than a teacher."

At the back of the room he could see the table laden with cakes and tea and it reminded him that his mother had once served in a school canteen before she had married his father. Again he was about to say something about her but refrained.

"I often used to think about those teachers who left the school. What happened to them? They went out into the great wide world but what happened to them after that? Did they disappear from human view? No, they did not. Their work lies here and also in the hands of those who work and teach and turn lathes in the furthest corners of the earth. Perhaps even there our work is remembered, over the whole world. In some steaming jungle, on some ship or other, in an office, in the furthest east, perhaps our words and our instructions are still remembered. That is what I think, and that is my faith.

"But do not forget that civilization is thin and fragile, that the barbarians are always beating at the gates, and we must be the guardians and the watchers, sentries at our posts as even Socrates was. As long as we exist perhaps night won't fall.

"When I came here first the pupils wore school uniform. Now they don't. These little things are significant, though some may not think so. When you think about it every little thing is significant. It is the addition of the little things that make up the quality of a civilization, and a school too is part of civilization, and is a leader and keeper of that civilization.

"My name is Trill, as you know, and on the whole I am an insignificant man. But I am the guardian of the works of men more significant than me. I am the casket for their works and their teachings and so I become significant. And the same is true of all of us. When I come into the room I am not just Mr Trill, I am Vergil and Homer as well. This, when you think of it, is a great honour. Of course in the tenor of my life I have done some petty things, perhaps to some of you. I may even have argued about the peg on which my coat was hung, but nevertheless beyond and behind all this I am the guardian of the best minds of the ages. Isn't that a frightening responsibility? Sometimes, as you know, children will almost break our hearts because they do not seem to be listening to what we have to say to them. But in the end we shall prevail because that is what we must do, there is no alternative. There were times when I didn't feel like coming to school in the mornings and some of you may have felt the same yourselves. But I came just the same because every minute counts.

"I had this sense of urgency as if it had been left to me to save the souls of our younger generation. Was that, do you think, egotism or pride? Perhaps it was. So, before I leave, I wish to say to you that we must have this urgency. I know that many pupils used to laugh at me and say, 'There is Mr Trill again, rushing along the corridor with his book open in front of him.' But why did I do that? It was because I did not wish to waste a minute, for the battle is continually around us. Sometimes its sound is muted by the concerns of the day, but don't believe that it isn't there and that many people don't live and die in that battle. It too has its victims and its victors. It too has its flags and its cohorts and its generals. I was never one of the generals, I would have described myself as a corporal or even a standard bearer. But that didn't bother me. The only thing that bothered me was, Will I be found at my post? Will I be a watchman?

"And that is the final message that I would like to leave with you. We must do what we can the best we can. Nobody can ask any more from us."

The speech ended to prolonged applause. However, though Mr Trill didn't hear them, there were criticisms. Morgan the Geography teacher for instance said,

"One would think he was Julius Caesar or Hannibal the way he talked. Everyone knows that he had no time for the dimwits, and these are the real test after all. He was lucky to have had the best of it. Coffee, Miss Scott?" He shook his hair back boyishly as he always did and Miss Scott said, "Tea for me, Mr Morgan. I thought you knew that."

During the brief meal the teachers talked about inflation, pay, bad pupils, shortage of accommodation, marks. Finally Mr Trill was left alone. When most of the teachers had left after saying goodbye to him, he himself slipped out. He walked along the empty corridors which the cleaners had already washed. His feet echoed with a hollow sound and it seemed to him that he was young again in that place which he had for so long inhabited. Voices returned to him from the dead, gowns rustled, the walls were clean and new again. He stood at the main door, pausing a moment before shutting it. Then he pulled the great ring of the handle behind him. As he walked across the playground it was as if he was dizzily coming into the world again, about to scream like a child which has just been born. He descended the steps and waited for the cars to pass. Then he crossed the road and went home to his lodgings.

"Who are you?" said Mr Trill as the figure emerged from the mist about him. But it did not answer, as it shyly gazed across the dark water.

Mr Trill felt a strange awe and ardour as if he were in the presence of a famous, almost divine man such as he had never seen in his life before. Head bowed, as if it were a monk, the figure studied the river with its fathomless modest eyes.

"I think," said Mr Trill, "I think you are Vergil himself." And he went down on his knees as if to a god. The dark water, the swirling mist, were about the two of them as they met in the faded light.

"I think," said Mr Trill, "by your silence and your modesty

that you are Vergil himself. I wish to tell you, I wish to tell you," he stammered, "that I think you are the greatest of all poets."

"*Sunt lacrimae rerum mentem mortalia tangunt,*" he said, "I think that is the greatest line of poetry that was ever written.

"The tears of things," said Mr Trill as he gazed at the figure with love and respect.

"That is all past," said Vergil. "That is all over now. My work was inadequate. In comparison with divine Homer my work was nothing."

"But the pity," said Mr Trill, "the pity, the divine pity."

"That too is over," said Vergil. "My trouble was that I could never write narrative. I should never have written of Rome. I was never a public poet. Better for me to have written of my farm. I should never have written of great events. What were politics to me?"

Gazing sadly across the waters he said, "I should have destroyed all my verse. It was not good enough. I did not have the divine sunniness of Homer and his good temper. The best I could do were set pieces. I substituted style for content. I was a decadent. All I wished was to be a private person."

"Did you not then get pleasure from writing?" said Mr Trill.

"Pleasure? It was the greatest labour that one can conceive of. Words slipped away from me. I could not keep them together. I was alone, polishing and polishing, refining and refining. How tired I was of Aeneas. Was he perhaps myself? If he wasn't myself who else could he be? Religious, correct, boring, what did I have to do with him? As one of your own poets has written, the task made a stone of my heart, I was tired of him. How is the founding of a country worth a lost love? How? I betrayed myself. Is Rome worth one broken heart? Tell me that. That is the question that has tormented me. Is the great task, the great hero, worth the lives of the innumerable dead?"

"I do not know," said Mr Trill.

"But is it? Think of it. Aeneas has to found Rome and what was Rome? Think of what it became, the games at which human beings were thrown to the lions while the emperors and the mob cheered in their bronze and their rags. Was that worth the death of one woman, one soul? How could I have written the words, 'But meanwhile Aeneas the True longed to allay her grief and dispel her sufferings with kind words.'

"I tell you, I grew tired of him. He should have forgotten about Rome. What was his duty but a terrible blindness? What are all our duties in the end but that? I betrayed myself as a poet. What were these boring battles to me when I wished to write about the human heart? What is history but the deaths that we need not share? That is why I wished the *Aeneid* to be burned because in it I had been false to myself. Do you understand? It wasn't the labour that I regretted nor was it the technical revision that I needed another three years for. Not at all. It was the central question that perplexed me and that I couldn't solve. On the one hand there is the founding of a great nation, which I believe in, yes, to a certain extent I believed in it, for after all what else was there to believe in? But I was seduced by the human and I understood that a great nation is built over the bones of men and women. Night after night I heard their cries as if they were trying to get in. My heart trembled and shook with their cries and their pain and their tumult. How could I write poems, how could I? How could I fashion lines in the midst of all that pain? Tell me that, whoever you are. Here at least however I have some peace. I do not wish to speak of my poems again, they shriek at me with their bleeding roots."

"No," said Mr Trill, "that isn't all there is, surely. Discontent everywhere. Discontent and smallness where one had thought was greatness."

"I should not have stayed so long in my study," said Vergil. "I should have gone out into the world that Homer knew. I should have lived off the justice of the moment. Do you understand?"

He was silent at the water, and then turned to Mr Trill.

"It is not that I wish to be impolite. How could I wish that? You too have had your life. Perhaps you have lived off the justice of the moment more than me though perhaps you aren't a poet. So few of us have the nerve and the power to do what I have just said we should do. A line a day, that is all I wrote, perfecting, perfecting. And all the time I had a vision that I should follow the curve of the human heart. All my work was but a feeble approximation to my ideal. As we stand here, by this dark water, what are empire and bronze to me? I have thought about this for a long time while I have been here. Up above, the empire no longer exists and when it did exist it was only a shade. My greatest terror is that I shall meet Dido. What should I say to her? Tell me, whose side was I on? I betrayed myself because I made a case for Aeneas when there was no case for him at all. None. What has the king to do with the poet, what has the empire to do with him? Nothing. What has power to do with him? I tell you I should have burned that book with my own hands."

As Mr Trill sat side by side with Vergil and gazed into the dark water it was as if he saw that all effort is vain, that all endeavour is without sense, that beyond statues and paintings and books there is the shadow of the dark stream which reflects nothing, thinks nothing and only is it itself.

"No," he shouted, "it is not true. Not true." And his eyes flashed as they had once used to do when he had entered the classroom with a copy of the Aeneid open in his hand while outside the window the traffic roared by. "No," he shouted, "there is something left. Something remains."

"What is it that remains?" said Vergil turning towards him his pale tormented face. "All that can remain is the human heart and how have we treated it? How have we written of it? We set up systems and so we avoid writing of it. We do not attend to the trembling, the fear, the music of the human heart. I was seduced by armour and war because I myself was unwarlike, and I did not see the trap into which I had been led. I forgot about the terrors of the living. Rome was a curtain that hid the truth I should have seen. The human soul, that is what is important, the infinite tenderness."

"And that you had," said Mr Trill. "Of all the poets that is what you had. The tears of things."

And he thought that in one way he at least was like Vergil, he had never married, he had suffered the silence and the dispossession, like a tree that stands by itself without leaves, bare to the wind.

"No," he shouted, "you have not failed. How could you have failed when so many centuries later I still read your works?"

But the figure, fatigued and insubstantial, had faded away into the mist and Mr Trill could no longer see it. "Dear God," he said, "what now is there left to me when even the author whom I loved best thinks that he has failed, when the heroes of my childhood turn out to be simple and egotistical men, when the monsters abuse the heroes for being hateful and aggressive. What is there left for me to do or say?"

And he sat with his case beside him on the bank of the river gazing deep into the dark water where no reflections were visible. Is the dark water the end of everything, he asked himself. Is that really true? The dark water where no fish lives, where no wave moves, where there is only motionlessness without end.

He gazed deep into the dark water and it changed as he looked, and he was lying in his bed again.

Mr Trill lay in his bed in the hospital staring at nothing. An old woman with a hoover was humming like a hornet round the ward. After a while Mr Trill began to study her. She had a scarf wrapped round her head and she wore a blue uniform and her nose was narrow and long. Where have you come from, thought Mr Trill, do you have children? When did you begin to work here? For some strange reason she reminded him of his mother, busy, distant, forever creating noise among the silence. Across the floor lay bands of sunlight, which streamed in through the window and among them the dust sparkled and moved as if it were alive. Through the windows he could see trees with golden leaves, and in the distance a moor which was turning brown. He lay in his bed knowing that he was going to die.

It all happened very suddenly. One moment he was reading in his room, the next his chest was a battlefield of pain which threatened to kill him. He had enough energy to knock on the wall before he fell. The next thing he knew he was in an ambulance and the next thing after that he was being operated on. A doctor was bending over him while he gazed upward at the ceiling. In a short while he was asleep.

The woman had now passed his bed and was hoovering the space in front of the next one. Mr Trill stared at the red blanket, at the man with the gaunt face who was lying under it, at the black grapes which lay beside him on the table. The man got visitors regularly, and Mr Trill got none except that his landlady came now and again. He would have liked visitors, even some of the pupils he had taught, even some of the teachers who had once been his colleagues, but no one came. It was as if he had already dropped into a big hole from which he could see no one, through which light would never again escape as the ring of gravity tightened.

So this is what death will be like, thought Mr Trill, and he was not frightened, only tired as if all the work he had done during his life had at last caught up with him. In fact sometimes he felt peaceful and content as if what was happening was happening to someone else, and not to him at all. Sometimes it was as if he was gazing down at himself from a position above the bed, and wondering what he was doing there. At night he could hear coughing, and nurses moved quietly through the dim light. Sometimes he would hear a man talking in his sleep, as if arguing with his wife or his employer.

There were bowls of flowers everywhere, not brought by visitors but donated by gardeners. There they stood brilliantly blossoming from the sparkling crystal, among the reds and white of the blankets and sheets. Now and again a nurse would pass with a trolley, and he would see her as a saviour among all the spit, blood, urine. At nights the nurses would laugh and shout as they entered a taxi on their way to a dance. Well, why shouldn't they enjoy themselves, how else could they remain sane, in a world of death and dying.

But now at this particular moment on this serene morning Mr Trill didn't feel at all frightened. It was as if like the season itself he was poised between growth and decline, blossoming and withering, as if his mind and soul were in balance, calmly accepting the justice that was about to come. I am about to die, he thought to himself, and this woman with the hoover will live, not forever, but perhaps for a long time yet. Perhaps her whole

life has been spent like this, cleaning and hoovering. She has
never aspired to anything else. I on the other hand wanted more,
I aspired to train minds in the great poetry of the ages. And what
use was it after all? Now I am alone and no one comes to see me.
Of all those thousands I have trained no one comes to visit me.
Well, let it be, let it be. The sunlight is indifferent to us all. We
are who we are and that is all that can be said about us. He
watched an old man, slightly healthier than himself, being
helped by two nurses out of his bed to sit in the lounge and watch
the coloured television. He would sit there all morning,
sometimes dozing off, sometimes staring ahead of him.

The old man tried to push the nurses away from him as if he
thought that he could manage quite well on his own. His face
was stern and bitter, as if he had not accepted what had
happened to him, even though he was old. Shall I be a coward,
thought Mr Trill, when I am about to die. Shall I thresh about
on the bed? He had never seen anyone die, not even his father or
his mother, and he didn't know what to expect. He wanted to
die quietly and tranquilly, like a Greek or Roman hero who
dispensed with life as if with a sword for which he no longer had
any use.

Steadily the hoover hummed and brightly the sun shone on
the floor. I never had time to notice this before, thought Mr
Trill. How did I not notice how the dust moves like insects, how
even the clearest sun contains a proliferation of dark grains?
Perhaps this very day will be my last, this serene autumn day
whose calmness is like that of great art, when all passion falls
away and only the essential fullness of things is left behind. On
this morning there was no "tears of things," no "*lacrimae rerum*,"
there was only an almost holy calm.

I have never made a will, he thought. What will happen to my
money? I have no one to leave it to. But he didn't care, the
survival of his money after him didn't seem to matter. And he
had saved a lot of money for he hardly ever spent any. There it
lay, symbols and signs in his bankbook, and he didn't care. It
was almost a joke, to leave all that complication behind. He felt
like an exile who was looking back at the world as at a strange

distant shore. The woman was now at the far end of the ward,
the flex of the hoover trailing behind her like a black snake.
  Mr Trill looked at the bed opposite. Above and behind it on
the wall there was a brass plate which said that the bed had been
donated by William Mason. Who now remembered him,
whoever he had been? Perhaps he had once been a rich man,
enthusiastic, competitive, red-faced, but now all that was left of
him was the name, read by an ignorant man. Our ignorance is
total, thought Mr Trill, our achievements minimal. We move
about the world as if we were important, we fight and squabble
over trivial things, we feel slighted when we are seated at the
wrong table, and yet in the end all these things are unimportant.
The universe is a huge, unimaginably huge, organism, in which
we are as important as the dust in the sunbeam, flickering
slightly and then fading from sight.
  The hoovering had ceased and the ward was silent. I am lying
here like an effigy, thought Mr Trill. Should I try to get up or
not? But he did not wish to get up. He wished to lie where he was,
resting, happy. The boy with the hole in his heart lay sleeping
peacefully opposite him, his fair hair strewn over the pillows. It
seemed unjust that he should suffer when he was so young.
  Mr Trill looked out of the window which was open. He saw
two boys throwing stones up into a tree so that the chestnuts
would fall down. When they did so they put them in a bag which
they were carrying. A minister with long hurrying strides passed
the window. The sky was perfectly blue without a cloud in it.
Early November was exact and accurate and clear. I am dying,
he thought, and I have never loved anyone and there is no one
who will grieve for me. My funeral will be bare and diminished.
  Yet I am not frightened. Isn't that odd? It is as if all the time I
was thinking not about myself but about someone else. He felt
his heart pattering, and listened to it as to an old friend who was
finally letting him down. Patter patter, hammer hammer, beat
beat. They say that the heart is the centre of love, but I have
never felt that. I never used to notice it much, it was there when I
needed it. Now when it is failing me I notice it. How much we
take for granted in this world, that we shall live forever, that our

bodies will remain our indefatigable servants. He remembered the oxygen tent, the hard serious breathing, but again it was as if he was thinking of someone else, as sometimes one may look at an early photograph of oneself standing on a sideboard and one may not for a moment recognize it. He felt his face which was stubbly and unshaven, like a field of autumn corn. He wondered what he looked like. His pyjamas felt larger than they had previously done, so presumably he had lost weight. The watch had disappeared from his hand. None of his clothes were to be seen anywhere. It was as if he had arrived in the final place where all must be confiscated, where the only values are physical, how much of flesh and bone and blood can still survive.

The ward was beginning to waken up. Now he could see a nurse examining a thermometer, thin and silver in the sunlight. Very faintly he could hear laughter from the lounge where the coloured television was. Soon perhaps they would get him out of bed and he would sit with the others staring at that oddly distant screen. The nurses would smile and laugh and joke, they would walk about with such great energy and speed, as if they did not wish their patients to have any time to think.

The world would assume the noise and din of normality. Nevertheless his heart was beginning to hammer again, as if a blacksmith were forging some new iron thing on an anvil of deep black, as if a train were accelerating steadily on an autumn day when the flowers are tall and red and wasteful beside the rusty rails. It was as if he was rocking from side to side down a forgotten siding. I am feeling dizzy, he thought, something is happening to me. Is this it then? Is that unimaginable pain going to pierce me again?

He waved frantically as no words would come out. The nurse continued to regard the thermometer as if it were a tiny silver fish she had caught and which she was studying for size. The rackety old train was bouncing up and down. Somewhere down there was a black tunnel which, when he entered it, would make the carriage dense and thick and dark so that he could no longer see the pictures on the wall, the blossoming flowers in their sparkling vases.

He waved again and someone came. Then they were all about him. A face was bending over him, fresh and young and inquiring. His face and that other face were very close, close enough almost to kiss. A hand was clutching at his own: he hung on as if he were clinging to the side of a raft. How marvellous, he thought, that we should help each other, that in spite of hatred and insult and anger there are those who rush to one's side when it is necessary. How marvellous that they are not simply professional people but that they expend their own precious store of love and pity on perfect strangers. How truly amazing the world is, how bad and how good, and how, in spite of all, more good than bad. It was now as if he was seeing flashes as from a tall lighthouse searching a dark sea. Steadily they came, then faster and faster.

At that moment it was as if he were a well full of water, of love, as if a full tide were rising inside him. I love you all, all you fallen ones, all you autumn ones. We are all in the same boat, but the lighthouse is sending out its flashes, mortal meagre hands are blessing me, hands which have curved round the handle of a hoover, examined a thermometer, emptied bed pans. We do not deserve such care, such love. In spite of their petty quarrels, their envies, the unambitious ones help one at the end. He felt tears slowly trickling down his face, and in front of him the young stunned inquiring face was also wet with tears. He wanted to say, It's not as bad as that. Though I'm dying I feel quite happy. Don't worry. The eyes were so dear and so fresh and so filled with light. They should not be seeing this, he thought. Then they were no longer there. There was nothing at all. And Mr Trill passed over into Hades.

Mr Trill was aware that the baying of the dogs across the other side of the water had ceased, and that a small boat was being rowed towards him across the water. When the boat had reached his bank, a figure signed to him to enter it. Mr Trill looked around him to see if the invitation was to someone else, but the figure, still without speaking, signalled to him more impatiently and, with his case in his hand, Mr Trill stepped into the boat. It did not take long to cross to the other side, and when they arrived the figure, unspeaking as before, led the way to the large building that Mr Trill could see crouched in the vague prevailing mist. They passed a quadrangle and entered the building by a large creaking door. As Mr Trill stood in the hall where the notice-boards were covered with notices, the figure silently slipped away.

As if knowing where he was, Mr Trill climbed the stair to the door of an office on which he knocked, hearing from an adjacent room the sound of typewriters. After a long pause a voice asked him to come in, and when he did so he saw that seated behind a desk there was a small harried man in a black coat.

"Ah, Mr Trill," said this man, "my name is Dubbins. I'm very glad to see you."

Mr Dubbins rose from his seat and strode forward, putting out his hand. Mr Trill laid his case down and shook the hand extended to him.

"You may go along to the staff-room in a minute," said Dubbins. "We are happy to have you. Very happy."

"I have been here before," thought Mr Trill, "or if I haven't it is very like a place which I have visited."

"You are surprised," said Dubbins, "but you need not be. We have various alternatives to offer you."

"Alternatives?"

"Naturally. You may stay with us which is one alternative."

"And the others?"

"Another is to go back to your earlier life and continue your work there."

"And?"

"The other is to go back where you came from."

"I see."

"There seems to have been a flaw in our organization. We should have picked you up earlier. Still, that can't be helped."

"What did the others do?"

"Most chose to stay."

"And what is done here?"

"Done? My dear fellow, nothing much is *done*. We read and discuss."

"I see."

"I think the best thing would be if I took you along. Do you not think so?"

"I don't mind."

The headmaster looked round the office as if to make sure that he had forgotten nothing, and then the two of them walked along a corridor till they came to another door on which the headmaster knocked. When they entered, the occupants of the room stood up as if they were flustered by the unexpected honour of the headmaster's visit.

"This is Simmons," said Dubbins, "and this Morrison, this is Andrews and this Burbridge." The names followed each other like a roll call, and finally Mr Trill ceased to listen. All of them had been reading books when he entered and he noticed that all the books were classics such as *The Iliad* or Catullus' poems.

Suddenly a small bald man began to speak. "Headmaster, I don't think this is right. The place is becoming overcrowded already. Why are we bringing in another candidate? Soon we shall not have enough room for ourselves and our books."

"This is Carter," said the headmaster, "and he is always complaining."

In a corner by himself there sat another man whose face twitched continually.

"That's Harris," said Dubbins, "his nerves are bad."

"Now," he said, "if you wish to stay with the rest you can do so. All you require is a seat. You will be able to get any books you like from the library, and read them and comment on them. Little discussions are held regularly. What's that? Ah, another of our storms."

Mr Trill could hear what seemed like hail beating against the window, and beyond it the howling of the dogs. Beyond both of these there was the weird distorted cry of many voices.

"What is that noise?" he asked.

"It is the hail," said Dubbins.

"And beyond that?"

"That will be the cry of the dogs."

"And beyond that again?"

"I do not hear anything."

Dubbins's bland composed face, turned towards him, seemed closed and distant.

"Am I to leave you here then?" he asked. "We feel that we should all be together and that we should look after our own kind."

Mr Trill looked down at the classics which were lying on the table and they seemed to him to be surrounded by storm and wind, shaking in the hail which beat on them. Otherwise there was silence in the room and all the other occupants, retired into the world of their books, appeared to have already forgotten about him.

"What did you say my choices were?" he asked.

"To stay here or go back to your life and teach there or go out into the place from which you came."

"Are there no other choices?"

"There is one other, but no one has taken it so far."

"And what is that?"

"To go back to life but not as a teacher. We allow this, but it is not a choice that we like anyone to take. That is why I did not mention it."

"Why don't you like it to be taken?"

"We think of it as an admission of failure."

"Failure?"

"We feel that it is an admission that what we are doing is not considered important."

"I see."

The man in the corner twitched uncontrollably.

Mr Trill looked down at a copy of Homer, then turned the pages idly. In the margin of the book there were pencilled comments. One said, "Ironical?" Another said, "An example of synecdoche?" A third one said, "The hexameter as narrative technique."

Suddenly as he was speaking an excited voice shouted, "I have found it. I have correctly dated the Georgics."

Heads turned towards the speaker simultaneously. One man said, "The fool. Who does he think he is? That has already been done by Malonivitz." Another said, "I shall have to rebut whatever he says."

The headmaster gazed smilingly at Mr Trill and said, "See? Nothing but excitement."

Mr Trill felt as if he was going to be sick. Even though the headmaster heard nothing he himself was hearing beyond the hail and the baying of the dogs the voices of many men shrieking in pain, cursing, tormented.

His mother stood at the door.

"Put that woman out at once," shrieked Carter. "She has no right to be here."

But his mother stood stolidly there.

"This is outrageous," shouted Carter. "What is this place coming to? Nothing but deterioration day after day. Standards failing, texts inadequate, and now we have women. I shall, I shall . . ." But foaming at the mouth he subsided for he could not finish the sentence.

Mr Trill thought of an army of synecdoches meeting an army of metonymies on a battlefield where vivid green and blue scarves waved. Ah, the billowing bronze of my unlived life! The wind that drives the similes before it.

But his mother had gone. She had lived among the little piercing needles of the day, stung, stinging.

"I shall go back," he heard himself saying.

"To Hades?" said Dubbins.

"No, to the world in which I once lived. I shall return as something else." There was a universal sigh of horror all over the room.

"As something else?" they sighed.

"Yes," said Mr Trill.

"Are you sure?" said Dubbins.

"Quite sure," said Mr Trill, "if it is possible, that is."

"But no one before has asked that he go back as someone else."

"In that case I shall be unique," said Mr Trill and he felt an odd pleasure.

"I shall go back without shield."

"Without shield?" They all gazed at each other as if he had said something incomprehensible.

"That is so," said Mr Trill. "Naked and without shield. I shall watch the wheelbarrows."

"What is he talking about?" they asked.

"The wheelbarrow and the stone," said Mr Trill. "With rain on it, perhaps sunshine. The train that travels through the day. The man who collects the tickets in his dirty blue jacket. The drunk in the restaurant. The Chinaman who dreams of Hong Kong. The lorry driver, the builder, the carpenter with the ruler in his breast pocket. The docker who heaves the cargo to the quay. The cloud that has lost its way, and to which the child points. The bin man who lifts the grooved ash can on to his shoulders. The lady standing at the corner with the neon light on her handbag. To all these things I pray, to the rain that falls, the sun that shines. To the temporary I give my allegiance."

Suddenly there was no room there at all and Mr Trill found himself standing at a windy corner in a vast city selling newspapers.

"*Evening News*," he was shouting. "*Evening News*." A man with a rolled umbrella took a paper, threw money on the ledge and then slanted quickly away into the lights of the city.

"*Evening News*," Mr Trill shouted. "Terrible murder, terrible rape. Read about it in the Evening News."

Men and women passed through the yellow lights. Mr Trill clapped his hands together in the cold. In the distance the high windows burned like stars and it seemed that they were all on fire, twinkling and guttering.

"*Evening News*," shouted Mr Trill in a sudden access of joy, ready to dance up and down on the pavement. "Read about the murder, the rape, the embezzling, the incest. Read about the rescue, the gift, the offer. *Evening News*, read all about it."

Around him the lights winked and shivered. His boots were yellow in the light, he crowed like a cock, his bronze claws sunk in the pavement.